Diamonds used to be this girl's best friend.

Jewelry designer Mary Keefe has been robbed--of a million dollars in diamonds

belonging to her grandfather--by her own boyfriend, Conrad. Besides recovering the jewels, she's got to conceive a baby within 5 days, to save her family's legacy. Her friends have a plan, a singles cruise so Mary can find a sperm donor with the best qualities. The first mate could be the right choice--he rates a five on the Donor List. Then there's John Wang, her neighbor in the adjoining room. Attraction sizzles between them and they've become friends, but he doesn't act interested. Could be, she's not his type.

For John Kajiyama, posing as Wang, Mary Keefe is just his type. She's beautiful, funny and sweet...but is she innocent? Diamonds are missing and he must recover them for the insurance company. How far will he go to maintain his cover in this investigation?

Books by j.j. Keller

Jewel Heist
Love Hurts

Published by Kensington Publishing Corporation

Jewel Heist

j.j. Keller

LYRICAL PRESS
Kensington Publishing Corp.
www.kensingtonbooks.com

Lyrical Press books are published by
Kensington Publishing Corp. 119 West 40th Street New York, NY 10018

Special book excerpts or customized printings can also be created to fit
specific needs. For details, write or phone the office of the Kensington
Special Sales Manager:
Kensington Publishing Corp.
119 West 40th Street
New York, NY 10018
Attn. Special Sales Department. Phone: 1-800-221-2647.

First Electronic Edition: October 2011
eISBN-13: 978-1-61650-327-7
eISBN-10: 1-61650-327-0

First Print Edition: October 2011
ISBN-13: 978-1-61650-880-7
ISBN-10: 1-61650-880-9

Printed in the United States of America

This book is dedicated to all women who want to become mothers.

Acknowledgements

I would like to thank my exceptional editor, Mary Murray. Medical advice was provided by health care worker, Kathleen Grieve. A special thanks to Ericka Scott, who is always there for me and stays honest and forthright. My appreciation to Tracy Scott for taking the cruise.

Chapter 1

The bag of uncut diamonds fell from the safe and poured into Mary Keefe's palm. She gaped in wonder. A million dollars' worth of Canada's finest, freshly mined from Whip Lake near Yellowknife. Slivers of ice appeared in the sharp edges, indicating what lay beneath the cool surface. She ran her finger and thumb over one of the chalky exteriors, anticipating what brilliant masterpiece she could create, devising a cut plan while envisioning a beautiful engagement ring.

"Mary, I'm taking off," Lisa said from the doorway leading into the sales room. "Dental appointment, remember?"

Mary sat at her desk and glanced at her part-time sales associate. Lisa's bejeweled hand perched on her slender hip, and in the bright lights of the cutting room, all of her sparklers came out to play. Mary had fashioned at least two of the baubles. Unable to resist, she tore her attention away from her co-worker and focused on the rough natural diamonds. "Oh. Okay, Lisa, I'll see you tomorrow."

"Do you want me to put the closed sign on the door and lock it?" Her tone held resignation. "Andre wouldn't mind having a bit of freedom from guard duty."

Mary laughed, fingering the soon-to-be resplendent stones. She must return them to their velvet nest. "You knew I'd be fascinated with the goods."

Lisa chuckled and glanced at her watch. "Sorry, it's too late to cancel the appointment."

"No, don't worry. I'll put these away and sketch designs between waiting on customers in the lobby."

A silvery blond eyebrow lifted. "You're sure?"

Mary nodded to the door. "Yes. Please, go."

Lisa took a step. "Good night. I'll see you after you return from your trip." She strode to the exit, her wide handbag flapping against her narrow side.

Mary sorted through nature's mysterious stones one more time. At the click of the door, she stashed the rocks inside their dark blue bag.

The shuffle of feet drew her attention from the sack's drawstring. Lisa must have forgotten something. Instead of her assistant, a tall thin man completely covered in black from his ski mask to leather shoes, swayed inside the room.

Her heart beating as fast as the second hands on the clock collection at the south side of the jewelry store, Mary moved around the desk, intending to stuff the pouch into the safe and slam the door. "Who are you?"

The intruder didn't deter her. However, the metal safe seemed farther away than it had appeared a moment ago. She crept forward, keeping the dark opening in sight. "My assistant will be back in a second."

An arm came out of nowhere and wrapped under her breasts, preventing her upper body from moving. Despite her breath expelling so fast it hurt, she hurled the stones and threw her head back, connecting with the chin of her attacker.

"Shit!" a man snapped. A familiar voice. Please, it couldn't be him.

The bag hit the rim of the safe with a thunk. As with all things earthly, the jewels fell.

She screamed loud enough surely her grandfather, in his office two stories up, would hear the vocal alarm. Where was Andre? God, she hoped he was okay. One huge hand completely covered her mouth and the other twisted her arm. Deep breaths brought scents, a mixture of plant fertilizer and pungent Axe cologne into her nostrils. Beneath the soft wool, she bit her lips, trying to keep them from trembling.

"Go!" he shouted, releasing her mouth. He reached for the dark blue bag of a million dollars' worth of jewels resting on the cream and gray tiled floor. His partner shuffled out into the lobby, and soon breaking glass rippled through the silence. Smoke billowed into the office. Damn, her new glass display cases, destroyed. Surely her grandfather heard the explosion and would come running.

Her teeth clung to her attacker's wrist as he bent, until his hand flipped and covered her nose and mouth, forcing her to relax. He stood straight, easing the tension of the hold. Velvet rubbed against her stomach where the blouse had come free from her slacks. They had made love once, on this very floor. An image of him placing a few minor gemstones on her belly and moving them around with his tongue flooded her mind. She resented the intrusion of a romantic tryst now that Conrad Peabody's true character had been exposed.

His gloved fingers continued to press against her mouth, jamming her teeth into the soft tissue. She finally got relief from the force when he moved his hand and used his teeth to pull off the glove. He stuffed the leather into his pocket, then transferred the bag of gems to his unencumbered hand. His breathing increased, pushing his chest against her back, as his fingers worked open the yellow binding of the casing.

Mary drew a sharp breath. There it was--the mole shaped like molar tooth--at the apex of his right thumb and index finger, confirming the identity of her attacker and thief--a dishonest, unfaithful, and untrustworthy lover. Conrad's sigh was followed by a sickly sweet scent, which tossed her into darkness.

* * * *

Two days later, Mary glanced at Dr. Kim O' Dell, at whose house her intimate group of friends had gathered. Kim closed her eyes, as if in thought. Phoenix Bushard, elementary teacher by day and karaoke star at the local Rock-On Bar and Grill, stared at Jenn. Jennifer Lucas was the most vocal of the beautiful threesome. Kim, Phoenix, and Mary had been friends since first grade. Years later, Jenn--Phoenix's college roommate--joined the group. They were comrades with such a tight bond, not even being accused of accessory to grand theft made their love for Mary falter. Her adoration for them increased in response to their faith in her, but she couldn't possibly rationalize what they intended for her to do. And if she did, following through with the plan would take a lot of courage.

DNA: Selective breeding.
Organs: In good shape.
Nice: Easy going attitude.
Outstanding: Gorgeous looks.
Resourceful: Intelligence is important in offspring.

Mary tapped underneath the last line on the white board with her blue erasable pen. "All of the donor preferences on this list are excellent and easy for me to remember, but I need a rating system of some sort."

"Right," Jennifer said, twirling her white-blond hair around a finger. *Snap! Crackle!* Her jaws were doing double-time on the chewing gum. Jenn's new attempt at not smoking was a challenge for all of them.

"Hey, Kim, why do you have an eraser board in your living room?" Jenn, with her usual bluntness, inquired.

Behind the white panel on the large stand-alone contraption with Kim's precise writing detailing the plan, the great expanse of twenty-foot windows gave them a sneak peek at the sun setting earlier than usual. A hint of fall was in the air. The other furnishings in the room were contemporary style, not her taste. Mary had suggested the mocha paint on the walls, which ran the length of the great room into the adjoining kitchen.

Kim's slender, light pink-tipped toes curled under her left leg and her other foot rested on her bent knee. Mary was envious, not only of her perfectly rail thin body, but her high cheekbones and dark russet hair rolling down her back in waves.

"It's new. We use it to help the kids with their homework. You'd be amazed how much after-school studying there is for six-year-olds these days," Kim said. Her children were gorgeous. Kim was so lucky to be able to conceive and give birth to the little girls.

"Let's focus on getting me impregnated before my last five days following the HCG injection passes." Mary recapped the blue pen and laid the dry erase marker in the trough. "I don't know if going on a cruise is the best method to find a sperm donor."

"I think it's amazing for someone who has a morbid fear of needles to get twelve hormone shots in the ass," Jenn said.

"Had to, and Conrad was by my side the entire time, so I had immediate support." Mary grimaced. "You can't imagine how much will power it took for me to go back that last time. At least I didn't see the needle coming. My tender bum felt like it was being attacked by killer bees."

"Not as much courage as it took to identify him as the robber of your store yesterday." Kim stirred her drink.

"Yeah. Can you imagine your partner taking you to get shots to procreate in the morning and stealing all of your untraceable diamonds a few hours later?" Jenn nodded.

"Back to the basics." Phoenix's periwinkle blue gaze focused on the words displayed. "This might be a mad scheme and she might not even find someone compatible, so let's keep her sorting agenda simple. How about a rating system from one to five, with the highest number being the best of the lot?"

Everyone nodded.

"Great, we're all in agreement." Mary chewed her tender, bruised lip and tapped the eraser board. "I must admit the donor chart is an innovative idea. I have a total of four days on the cruise. The first three will be used for sorting the prime from the slime. How do I ask questions to try and find the right candidate to provide safe sex without scaring him off?"

She had one chance. Her fertility doctor had spelled her current situation out very clearly. If she didn't conceive within the next week, because of the Razor family curse, she'd have less than twenty percent future viability. Her Grandfather Keefe threatened to shut down the business and sell her ancestral home if she didn't get married and provide an heir within a year. The store might be gone, but could she save her home? She had four months left to get pregnant. Half that if her percentage of viable insemination time decreased.

A baby. More than drawing her next breath, she wanted a child.

Six months ago she'd had a miscarriage, so her OB/GYN suggested a fertility regimen. Conrad had agreed, quickly and without blinking. He'd probably thought he wouldn't be caught robbing her store, and they'd go on the cruise and get pregnant as if nothing unusual had happened.

Mary uncapped the marker and held the dark tip under the first line. "This one is self-explanatory. Organs?" She glanced at Kim. "You're the doctor. Tell me what type of questions I should ask to get the most from the query?"

"Well, if you're going to catch an eligible guy unaware, why not ask him about his habits?" Kim rubbed her chin, deep in thought. "If he has a good physique, his overall health will be obvious. If you see a man who drinks alcohol like a fish, I'd wonder about his ability to cope. His liver might not be in the greatest shape, and alcoholism might run in his family." She stood and paced from the white board to the edge of the family room. "Over dinner or lunch, it will be easy to ask questions about his family history. Heredity is where the risk factors really lie and are those that can't be changed. Especially when it comes to heart disease and stroke--"

"And?" Jenn interrupted.

"The trick will be to ask as many questions as you can in a casual manner and store all the information in your notes later. If possible you need to search his luggage for any drug use. I'll write down meds associated with HIV and other diseases. You should abandon unsafe sex if you see any of those," Kim finished.

"Mention your aunt provided the cruise because she died from heart failure. A few tears would be good," Phoenix suggested.

"Yeah, every person I've ever talked to when an illness is mentioned, they have a comeback story." Jenn flapped her thumb and fingers, imitating talking.

"The longer they rattle on, the higher number, and five will be a negative." Phoenix removed her hair tie, pulled her light brown hair into a fresh tight ponytail, and bound the mass into a knot again.

Jenn squinted. "Maybe she'll keep the same rating system for all of the categories, with one being the negative, like the guy who yammered on and on."

"Do you think this is a cold-hearted way to create a family?" Mary bit her uninjured lip. Kim was right; needing to filter as much as possible from each candidate would be nerve-wracking and time consuming. Time wasn't her ally. Her heart clutched as she remembered her doctor's advice on getting pregnant. There wouldn't be a better time than now. The future looked grim. Yet, shouldn't a child be made from love, and not from a tube or a guy she'd only just met?

"No, think of it as the guy is a vessel, holding jewels. You're simply going to heist them." Jenn tapped her fingers on the top of her thigh.

"No she's not," Kim said. If the circumstances weren't so gloomy, Mary would have burst out laughing at her aghast expression.

"Uh huh. Five-fingered discount." Jenn pumped her hand in front of her pelvis.

"You're disgusting. She's going to get consent before having unprotected sex." Phoenix glanced at Mary, as if to ask "right?"

"Yes. Of course I will," Mary replied, while quickly reevaluating the plan.

"Look for yellow too, in the eyes, a faint tint to the skin. Yellow isn't a good color for health. It means something's wrong with his liver or bile duct." Kim unlatched her leg and stood. She wiggled her toes in the plush cream carpet. "I'm going to get a T. Sunrise. Anybody else?"

"Me," Jenn called from her position near the white board. She wrapped her gum in a slip of paper.

Phoenix rose. "I'll take a coffee. I have a late night grading papers." She trailed Kim into the sunny kitchen adjoining the family room.

"Nice will be easy to judge," Mary said, loud enough to be heard over the ice dispenser.

"You can't believe in the niceness of most people. Guys, especially on a single's cruise, will be agreeable simply because, well, for obvious reasons--"

"What would that be?" Jenn's sly expression got her a frown from Phoenix.

"They're looking for an easy hook-up. Which will work in your favor," Phoenix said.

"So, I'll need to bash his favorite football team to get a rise?" Mary lifted an eyebrow. "Seems kind of mean."

"Or heckle him during his karaoke," Jenn added, as she walked into the kitchen and tossed her gum wrapper into the trash bin. "Like we do Phoenix after we've had a few drinks."

"I know it makes me pissed off," Phoenix muttered.

Mary joined them at the bar. In an effort to keep the space open, there was a small separation between the family room and the kitchen. Jenn had perched on the chrome bar stool. Kim was adding grenadine to a highball glass filled with tequila and orange juice. Mary glanced at each of them, noting they were mesmerized as the red syrup floated and eventually filtered down, creating a crimson base with the sun above. Kim held an acrylic stirrer. The flamingo's pink head became the handle to swirl the liquid, creating a sunset effect. "Here you go, Mary, your drink is alcohol free 'cause we don't want to mess with the hormone jive."

Mary slid onto one of the stools and took the tall glass. "Thank you. No alcohol for me for quite some time if I get pregnant. Really, I haven't missed drinking. Let's talk DNA. How do I get down and dirty, finding out if the guy has good genes?"

"If we had opportunity and time was on our side, we'd get a genetic screening done, but that'll take longer than your cruise. I'd ask some key questions about longevity, color, basic metabolism. Ask to see photos on his phone. Make sure you get to see family members and not old girlfriends." Kim sipped her exploding sunrise.

"So, she's to ask how long life expectancy is in the family and if there are multi-cultural elements?" Across the counter, Phoenix mixed cream into her coffee.

Mary looked at Kim, waiting to see her reaction.

"Depends on what's important to her." Kim's blue eyes lifted from peering into her glass. "You can ask questions without being direct. You can say your mom took a lot of pills, which worried you because you don't know what they are. They'll probably describe tablets to you, because of what they're taking. Text me and I'll tell you what it's probably used for."

"Good. Color or sexual preference isn't important to me. I mean, I want a straight guy to do me, but if he has relatives who've chosen a different life style, that won't affect my decision to select him as my baby's father." Mary stood, nodded in confirmation, and started to pace.

"Damn straight. If a guy has good genes and no signs of illnesses, he's a viable candidate." Jenn pulled her hair into a loose knot and then got a fresh piece of gum from her purse.

"Which brings us to another reason we wanted to get together." Phoenix sat at one of the bar stools, lowered her java and extracted a slip of paper out of her pocket. "We met earlier today."

"Because?" Mary's stomach churned. Her heart beat as fast as Jenn chomped on her new wad of gum. It had taken her friends' constant badgering for the past twenty-four hours to get her to agree to the cruise. The day before, she'd anticipated getting pregnant by the love of her life, and instead he'd robbed her store. The police couldn't find him or his partner in crime. Her bags had been packed for over a week, so she could pick up and go, but should she? Mary continued to have doubts about the ethics and even the possibility of getting pregnant with a stranger.

Phoenix held out a business card. "Here, take this."

Her sly expression bothered Mary a little. The paper was a business card. "Your brother in Vermont? Are you trying to tell me if it doesn't work out, he'll provide the sperm?"

A deep, throaty chuckle rippled from Phoenix as she released the card into Mary's open palm. "I think his life partner would have issues. What we want--"

"We think you need to have an out-clause." Jenn leaned on the black speckled granite counter.

"Out-clause?" The card crunched between Mary's fingers as her mouth dropped open.

"Considering *he* arranged this cruise to act out a sex-with-stranger fantasy, odds are he will try to get to you." Kim's no nonsense tone vibrated through the room. "Don't get nervous, Mary, but we think since your ex-boyfriend continues to be on the lam and considered dangerous by the cops, you might want to have an escape route if he should show up at one of the ports where you dock."

Mary fell onto the seat of the red plaid sofa. "Conrad would not go on a ship. He'll be caught by the police for sure."

Jenn snapped her gum. "Mary, I love you, so don't take this the wrong way, but you always choose handsome but stupid boyfriends. Most definitely Raddy-Boy would be likely to follow you on the cruise or wait for you to disembark and try to--"

"Jenn!" Phoenix shouted. She sat beside Mary. Phoenix's lips relaxed and her eyes softened, almost giving the impression of intense sympathy. Mary's heart rate escalated, she didn't want to hear what was to come. "Honey, we're your best friends and we have to tell you over the years you've selected…not the brightest guys to date."

"Bill, the pothead," Jenn said.

"Pete, the fertilizer salesman." Kim sighed.

"Jeremiah, the poet. Thomas, the artist." Phoenix patted Mary's hand.

"Tom and I were in the same design class. He wasn't dumb." Mary had to at least defend one of her choices.

"Austin, the waiter, was definitely the most handsome of all of them." Jenn spit her gum into a piece of paper and zeroed in on the shiny silver trash container a few feet away.

No one spoke. What were they waiting for? Did they think she'd agree her partner choices were idiot pretty-boys? She threw her shoulders forward and took a deep breath. Yes, she had chosen wrong.

"Clearly Conrad wasn't brainless. It took some intelligence to arrange to steal a million dollars of uncut diamonds and point the blame at me." Heat rose to Mary's face. She hated saying the words out loud. Her friends had kindly ignored the subject during dinner and most of the night.

"Oh, honey." Phoenix wrapped her arm around Mary's shoulders and gave a gentle squeeze.

Her goal, to become the most sought-after jewelry designer in Keefe, South Carolina, had been achieved. She'd stayed at the top for a mere year, until she met Conrad Peabody. How could someone with such a proper name have fooled her so severely? Her mistakes didn't deserve tears.

"Conrad was hot. I adored how his bright blond hair constantly fell onto his forehead. I loved his dimples, a charming set resting on the top corners of his mouth. He was built, perfect V." Mary leaned against the sofa.

Phoenix shifted, before her arm got trapped.

"How can you possibly talk about him in a positive way? Andre is still in the hospital, with a complex concussion. You had to shut down your store while the investigation is going on, because Peabody stole your jewels." Kim slurped the sunrise until nothing was left but crushed pink ice. "Thank God your grandfather arrived a few minutes after the robbery, or you'd have been tied up until a customer came in, or Lisa."

"I don't know, I guess because Conrad was beautiful. Maybe he was forced into stealing." This thought had been recurring since the entire ordeal began. The incident had to have been some sort of mistake. Didn't it?

"What do you mean, you don't know?" Jenn stood in front of Mary, looking a bit like a dark Peter Pan. "He was the leader."

"We'd been together for almost a year. Other than ditching me a couple of times, he was a perfect gentleman." Mary had to breathe. Her heart tapped little beats against her chest. "I loved him. I thought he loved me too."

"Hello, part of the con-artist personality. Get in, pretend to be someone else, steal and escape. I thought you understood that by now?" Jenn's snarky tone must have alerted her to the need for a new jolt of nicotine because she stomped away and withdrew another patch from her purse. As an attorney's office assistant, her knowledge of criminal activity and the law was priceless, but it came with a lot of stress. In addition, she and her husband had decided to start a family, which had encouraged Jenn to stop smoking.

"Okay, we know he had attributes. But overall, he stole from your place of business and made it appear you were to blame." Phoenix rubbed Mary's arm, gentle little circles that reminded Mary of how she soothed Kim's girls when they'd been hurt.

Mary put her drink on the side table and held her palms to her eyes, pressing so the pain would stay away. Everything her friends said was factual. She had to admit the truth and move past this entire ordeal. "Which is why this sperm-seeking cruise will be perfect. I'll get a baby without the blind fallacy of love."

"You'll need to hear the rest of the out-clause before you leave to jump on the boat." Kim withdrew a notebook from the sofa table. "Phoenix, you have the best penmanship. Write down the donor list and what the acronym stands for."

Kim met Mary's gaze as if she sought the truth. "Do you still want to have a child?"

Mary lowered her hands to rest on the top of her thighs. *Last chance* kept repeating in her head. "You all know my grandfather's edict. I haven't saved enough money to buy my house. It's the only thing of value left from my parents. The job, I can get one anywhere. I'd miss being my own boss and I love the store, but the building isn't as important as the memories inside my home. If I want to keep my life the way it is, then yes. I need to have a baby and hope Grandfather won't care about the marriage first."

"Okay then. You'll leave from Port Authority in about an hour. After the second full day, you'll disembark at Kingston. Then, you'll stop at the big island. I think it's called Port Yama. You'll find out straightaway if slime ball is on the ship because he'll find you. If he is, you jump ship at Kingston, seek out Sasha Framee. His name and phone number are on the back of this card." Kim handed Mary the card. "He'll get you on a plane or boat to Vermont."

"Go to my brother's house in Cage, and he'll hide you in his guest cottage." Phoenix sat down on the edge of the sofa. "Once we're notified you had to run, we'll go to Jenn's friend, Hotel Director Stubbing, who works on the ship. He can let us know what happened. As hard as it'll be for all of us, we'll have to stay away because Conrad had a partner and we don't know what he looks like…right?"

"Right, no one knows who he was. Conrad kept at my back the entire time and I didn't see any skin on the accomplice, just black clothing from head to toe. I recognized Conrad's voice, scent, and then the molar shaped mole on his hand. The hidden camera showed Conrad, but not a clear view of the other guy. They did get a voice imprint from the store's security equipment. He sounds a little like Darth Vader." Her throat had closed, making breathing difficult.

The entire situation was really too much. She should stay at home and hide out like she'd been doing for the last several hours. Why hadn't she canceled the cruise after Conrad betrayed her, stole from her and left her blind-folded and tied to a chair?

"James Earl Jones is the voice. Deep. Husky, kinda sexy," Jenn said, "like a smoker. God, I wish I had a cigarette." She jumped up and paced to the edge of the family room and then to the white board.

Phoenix handed Mary the diary containing the donor list. "Calculate the averages and select the best candidate. You have four days for optimum fertilization. Make them count. Probably research the top of your list for two days, select the father for your baby, and let the little spearheads swim the next two days."

"You're going to have to act a part, Mary. You can't be prissy or let guilt ride you. Most important of all, send snap shots of the finalist if you get a chance." Kim winked.

"I'm not sure I can be a scientist like you, Kim. I do feel guilt and I'm not sure I can select a guy to impregnate me using such a cold and callous scientific method."

"How do you think women select a sperm donor from a bank?" Jenn asked. "The only difference is you get to see the real guy. Unfortunately, you have to do the screening process. Also, having unprotected sex with a near stranger will be risky."

Mary slipped Dane Bushard's business card inside the journal and pressed it against her chest. "Maybe I shouldn't go. My destiny might not include children or love."

Kim was right on with the guilt comment. She couldn't tell the candidate her intentions or they might not perform, thinking she had ulterior motives. Yeah, she had motivation--she wanted a child. Did this make her an unlikable person?

"Sweetie, we didn't mean for you to abandon the donor project. We simply want you to be safe," Phoenix said, sincerity flooding her words. "We included an escape bag with a pay-as-you-go phone inside in your luggage."

Mary forced a smile. "Who knows the man in Kingston?"

"I do." Jenn had added a new piece of gum and chomped. "He's an old friend. Quite a nice guy. Clean, good looking, family dates back to the early Jamaicans…and the organs were all in working order."

Kim laughed. Phoenix's body jiggled with suppressed mirth.

"What?" Jenn's expression was one of surprise. "She only has two days on the ship before she ports, she might need a last chance." Jenn pressed her lips together as if in thought or recapturing a memory. "He's not blond, but he's hot, handsome, and quite skilled with his tool. He has the sexiest wink, slow and deliberate. I get orgasmic just thinking about him."

"Thanks, Jenn, I'll keep that in mind." Mary glanced at the board and then her friends. What if she couldn't get pregnant? Being the last member of the Keefe family might not be too bad. The town's name, Keefe, would last forever even if the descendants died off.

When she reached thirty, she'd inherit her trust money and could adopt a baby. She stood. A guy to hold at night, to kiss, and take to dinner or the movies--she didn't need one. Abandoning the cruise would be very easy to do.

"Don't, Mary." Phoenix's low tone drew everyone's attention.

Of all Mary's fabulous friends, Phoenix knew her the best and had always delved into her mind and found her weak points. Mary started for the door, notebook in hand, handbag in sight.

"Don't what?" Jenn asked between snaps and crackles.

Phoenix must have known Mary was ready to bolt. "She thinking of canceling. Get her luggage, Jenn. Kim, gather her purse, wrap, and make sure she has sun screen. Mary, is your cell fully charged? We're taking you to the ship and getting you on board early."

Kim twisted Mary around, grabbed both her arms and shook her. "Mary, you've had a rough way to go so far, losing your parents in that horrible manner and then being used by Conrad. Why not take control of your life, your future? You want a child, right?"

The mention of her parents brought a fresh pain to her heart, and her stomach muscles clenched.

"Yes." She lowered her gaze. Selfishness wasn't something she was comfortable with or wanted, but she needed a baby to make her life whole again.

"Forget everything then. Don't think twice about commitment and your usual strict values. Look past the blonds. And as always, we'll be here for you." Kim hugged her.

Jenn's arms circled her from behind. Phoenix came from her side and pushed her cheek against Mary's. Excitement and fear shocked her heart into beating at a scary-fast rate. If she couldn't conceive a baby, at least she'd have the most caring friends on earth.

"Let's go." Jenn stepped back and tugged Mary's vest.

"Okay, but we say good-bye in the car. You drop me off. I'll find my way to the cabin. I'll keep in touch daily. When possible, photos will be sent." Nauseous saliva wet her mouth. She swallowed, trying to keep everything in place as they rushed from the house and piled into Kim's van.

A traffic accident on the highway made the short drive much longer. Police vehicles and fire trucks blocked the street at nine PM. There wasn't an alternate route. The ship sailed at ten, and while they chewed their fingernails waiting for the emergency squads to leave, they reviewed the donor requirements. Finally the road patrol created a round-about and they rushed to the dock. Kim drove her vehicle as close as possible to the structure, hoping the Port Authority would not give her a ticket.

"Any minute that horn's going to blow. You'll to need to hustle. Too bad you wore the sexy five-inchers, your feet are going to hurt like hell."

"Jenn, seriously, is it time for another patch?" Phoenix asked, as she climbed into the rear of the van and extracted Mary's luggage.

"Thank you, all. I love you. Wish me luck!" Mary slid from the seat, holding her large purse close to her side, knowing the shield wouldn't protect her from the future.

Phoenix set the suitcases on the ground, and then hugged her. "Don't worry, it'll all work out. You'll be happy," she whispered before she let her go.

"We'll see, won't we?" Mary asked. The towering ships rising above the outline of the buildings were ominous. She grabbed her bags, gathered courage, and entered the check-in station. The passenger terminal was an outdated structure, beige covered with rust, not what Mary had expected from one of the most beautiful harbors on the coast.

"Are you with Verbena Cruise?" a sweet round woman with merry blue eyes asked. Her white name badge had *Mary* embossed in black.

"Yes, I'm Mary Keefe. Sorry I'm late. There was an accident."

Cruise Mary flipped through a stack of papers. "Good name. I'll get you squared away and give you the key card to enter the ship and your stateroom, but you'll need to carry on the luggage."

A few moments later, her bag was going into a scan machine. The attendant sorted through several documents to verify Mary was who she claimed to be. Finally, the papers had been nodded over and approved. Her luggage had dropped off the conveyor belt. Before she could change her mind, she grabbed the bag and ascended the gangway. It felt more like walking the plank. A few stragglers were strolling along the ramp. Passengers leaned over the railing, waving to their friends and loved ones.

The larger than life whistle blasted, vibrating the wooden platform as she scanned her card and went onboard. On deck, she dropped her bag to the floor.

"Welcome to Verbena Cruise lines. May I have your name?" The uniformed attendant--Purity, according to her name badge--held a clipboard with pen in hand. Her voice sounded chipper, but her face looked angry. Maybe her expression was a result of the tight white uniform pulling apart at the bust line.

"Mary Keefe." She held onto the railing as the gangway was disengaged from the ship.

"You're on Deck Eight, Oceanview Ninety-eight. Take the elevator around the corner." Purity pointed to her left. "Up one flight, turn right, four doors on the left."

"Thanks."

Mary snapped the handle of her wheeled case. The sound of it locking in place was lost in the noise of the ship's motors grinding and whinnying. She tugged her luggage down the corridor, around to the elevator. Most of the passengers must have been unpacking or celebrating setting sail because no one waited on the lift and it arrived in a moment's call. A finger to the Deck Eight button, and the doors closed.

A whoosh and ping later, she'd arrived. She glanced at the locator map on the outside of the elevator. Right looked to be the correct route. Handbag settled on the handle of her wheeled luggage, she started down the corridor. A pleasant baritone voice came over the speaker as the ship tilted toward the ocean. She double-stepped to the left.

The announcement became background noise as she rocked from one side of the aisle to the other. An older man started to exit a room when the ship shifted again. Mary took the opportunity to fly down the carpeted passageway until she located Ninety-eight. While dragging her purse closer, intending to remove her bag and snap the handle in to get a tighter grip on the luggage, the door opened. The ship tilted portside.

Mary jolted forward, smashing into something hard covered by soft cotton and smelling of spice. Propulsion sent both of them down, to land partially on the sofa. The thud of her plastic luggage hitting the wood floor blasted through the air. Mary glanced into his face. Handsome. Brown-black hair. Sharp cheekbones. Her purse clung to her forearm, snagging the tail of the guy's shirt along the way and exposing a good portion of tight, dark beige skin. From the way his body fit snug against hers, they were equal in height. He weighed in at…a little heavy. Muscle mass? She'd have to wait and see him in a bathing suit to find out. He smelled delicious, like those hot cinnamon nuts she loved to eat.

Lifting her gaze to his face, she stared into his dark brown sparkling eyes. "Sorry, I guess I don't have my sea legs yet."

"Definitely off to a rock hard start," he replied, but didn't bother to separate from her.

Chapter 2

John couldn't move. Somehow during the collision, her purse had attached itself to his shirt button, limiting his mobility. The woman's softness sank into the length of his body. Lush curves and warm, succulent heat made him lose his focus on why he was aboard the ship. The fragrant scent of wisteria had filtered through the air as she'd hurled them onto the sofa. He had to keep both feet grounded to the floor.

Her eyes, the color of fresh seaweed, widened, then her glance connected with his. "I'm supposed to be in Ninety-eight."

She waved her hand, the key card's silver band shining under the artificial light.

He gave in and shifted to the side. Had she noticed the painful rise beneath his zipper?

The purse strap, wrapped around her wrist, followed. She gripped the chain and tugged, agitating the beast below. He grabbed her hand and flipped the room key around, placing the large writing in front of her eyes. "Mary Keefe, Stateroom Ninety-six, Deck Eight."

"Damn, flaky greeter told me Ninety-eight."

He released the card and she lowered her hand to rest on his side.

John had considered the assignment a cake walk. The girl had arrived, to a semi-confined area. He'd secure proof of obvious fraudulent insurance practice and possibly gain information regarding the location of the diamonds, all the while protecting her--if needed. Mentally reviewing the data file he'd collected before he'd started his on-site investigation, he now understood. Mary Keefe was gorgeous, charismatic, and innocent-looking. All the characteristics, making her appear not guilty of grand theft.

A fascinating and beautiful red glow crept from her neck onto her cheeks, giving her a hot, desirable appearance. His arousal stiffened making his trousers seem much too snug.

Lips pressed tightly, she said, "If you move, I'll go to my room."

"Your purse chain is stuck to my shirt." He lifted the edge of his dark blue polo. "John, by the way. John Wang."

"Oh, sorry. I'm Mary Keefe from Keefe, South Carolina." She slipped her arm from the purse and sat up and away from him. Her dark green pants matched the little vest-type blouse she wore. The top didn't have sleeves and her arms were muscular, very sexy. His gaze was drawn to the valley between her breasts. The satin material slipped lower to the point where a mound slid into touch range. His cock pulsed.

Delicate work was needed to get the purse chain off his shirt without tearing the material, and John knew she had the skill.

John tugged the bag close and pulled the shirt around. When he shifted on the sofa, the chain jangled, adding background noise to the people walking in the hallway. The entrance door was propped open by her luggage, with the wheels in the corridor. "Maybe you should move your bag inside, so people won't trip."

Mary glanced at the exit. Traffic had increased since the ship had leveled out. Her long, slender legs untangled from the lotus position. She hurried forward. A quick jerk to her bright red luggage and the clack of the handle sounded. As she crossed the threshold, the door whooshed and snapped shut.

Her short slacks were huggers with no visible panty outline. His head whirled with the fantasy possibilities her beauty created. He'd worked a tiny hole in his shirt, making the ring more attached than before.

"Let me help." She sat on the sofa, legs crossed Indian style. The moment she leaned forward and took the purse and his shirt in hand, John's throat dried to the point he couldn't swallow.

Mary, focused on the task, apparently did not notice his discomfort. He tried to look at everything, think about anything except whether she had any undergarments on at all and how he'd fit nice and snug inside her. Didn't work.

He studied her, not that he needed to. He'd memorized every aspect of her life and every feature of her face. Her soft, nearly perfect body had been a welcome surprise.

"There you go. It's left a small hole, but that can be stitched." She threw the bag over her shoulder. "How about after I unpack, we go get a drink?"

He wasn't surprised by her invitation. They were on a cruise designed for hook-ups. "Sure."

She rose, smiled enough to show straight bleached teeth, and grabbed her baggage. "I'll see you in about thirty minutes?"

"Okay. I'll come to your place this time." He smiled. Not going into the field very often made him happy. He was a tech guy and former police detective. He'd done his time on the street. However, his knowledge of gems made him lead investigator for his case. If not for the ice, John Kajiyama, aka John Wang, would be sitting at a desk at Atlantic Coast Investigations in Florida right now. Instead, here he was, salivating over a stunning possible criminal.

He rose and followed her like a panting dog, waiting as she maneuvered the key card into the lock next door and flung the entrance open.

"See you in a few, John," she said and slipped into the room. Her shiny taut calves highlighted by the sleek black heels disappeared from sight.

His cock pressed against his jockeys. Any more stimulation and he'd crest. Christ, if he was this turned on by the mere sight of boobs and ankles, how could he lead an investigation? How long since he'd been with a woman? Clearly, too long.

* * * *

Mary leaned against the door and took a deep breath. His rock-hard penis had bumped nicely against her hips. Was he attracted to her, or was it a coincidence? Of course, any straight guy probably got a hard on when a woman was plunked right on his lap. He could have taken the angry approach. Instead he'd been nice, let her get her bearings, and saved the chain of her purse when it would have been easier to snap it apart. Perhaps she should have a buddy for the cruise? A plan formed. To keep on track, she'd repulse the undesirables by claiming she was with John. He could do the same with her, and they'd go their separate ways at the end of the night.

The next day would be spent entirely at sea. She could gather a lot of intel for a variety of candidates. Late afternoon the following day, they'd dock at Kingston. Either she'd need to escape--shivers coursed over her at the thought that Conrad could be onboard or at the port--or she'd invite one of the lucky men to sight-see with her. A little romp among the banana plants sounded like a pleasant time. She dragged her luggage forward and placed the canvas and plastic on a twin mattress. About a foot of space was between the two beds. Small size--she bounced on the mattress of the other--but comfortable.

The square port window was dark. Stars splattered the night sky, giving wondrous illumination to all who glanced upon their glory. Love happened under the stars, didn't it? She so wanted to have some connection to her baby's father, instead of a wham, bam, thank you, sir. Well, fate had stepped right up and shattered that dream. Imitation love had taken several months to develop with Conrad and that relationship had bombed. Injected with a total stranger's fluid by artificial insemination seemed cold and scientific. Phoenix had two students in her class who were brother and sister because the moms had used the same sperm donor. The teens hadn't known that when they were making out in the parking lot of the Lyon's Food Mart. It would be horrible to have one child who unknowingly fell in love with their brother or sister. Maybe the donor plan was the best alternative.

Somewhere in her bag, her cellphone rang. She unhooked the magnetic latch and dragged the tiny device into her palm.

Phoenix, the worrier. "Hi, just wanted to make sure you made it on board and wondering if you've run into anyone exciting yet."

"Funny you should ask. I was looking for my cabin, a door opened and I steamrolled a guy in the room next to mine." Mary unzipped her suitcase and began disassembling the contents.

"Way to go, girlfriend. Is he a viable candidate?"

"What? I want to know, too," Jenn said, her voice coming from a distance.

"Just a second." Phoenix repeated the story. "I'm going to put you on speaker phone in order for our addicted friend to hear."

"I don't think he meets the donor classification. Black hair, my height or an inch taller maybe, okay body. He's a nice guy." Her undies and sexy night garments went in the top drawer for easy access.

"I thought we weren't going to rule out browns or blacks in hair color?" Kim asked.

"I'm not."

"It's because he's short," Jenn shouted.

"No, if I wore flats he'd be taller than me."

"What are the problems then, bad DNA?" Kim asked.

"Nooo. I guess I'm not attracted to him." Mary sat on the edge of the bed and glanced at the bedside clock. "Not to be rude, but I need to go. I promised John I'd buy him a drink."

"No alcohol, Mary," Kim said.

"Bye," Mary disconnected and quickly hung up her limited wardrobe. The miniature dresser didn't pose a problem, because when a girl anticipated a sudden exit, she packed light.

The luggage wouldn't fit in the bottom of the cabinet, and considering the cabin was the size of her closet at home, she didn't want it to take up space. The bag wouldn't wedge sideways, lengthwise or vertically into the cupboard. Nothing worked. By now her hair had fallen from the loose bun at the nape of her neck, irritating her. She tucked the strand behind her ear as a firm rap sounded on the entrance.

Damn. She dragged the case to the connecting door and hung the strap over the handle, twisting the knob to make sure it was locked. Another rap, louder than the first, drew her attention. She ran and pulled the portal open. John stood outside.

"Hi, sorry, trying to squeeze the luggage in the closet. Didn't work." She cocked her head toward the large red rectangle dangling from the door knob. His gaze moved across her forehead, along her neck and down to her heaving chest. She resisted the urge to pull the material of her vest closed, preventing his perusal. As his brown-eyed glance met hers, his gaze darted around her face. Maybe her makeup was running down her cheeks. She did feel sticky. Stomach fluttering, she tossed a long strand of hair over her shoulder.

"I'll get it to fit." Instead of looking at the suitcase, his stare remained on her.

Why did she get a strong idea he wasn't referring to the baggage? At the titillating thought, a tingle started in her lower abdomen. Sexy verbal innuendo was her favorite type of sparring.

"Okay, I need to freshen up a little." Why the hell did her heart skip a beat? Watching him watch her, she missed the step up to the bathroom. Grabbing the handle, she awkwardly slipped inside. She'd tossed her cosmetic bag on the counter as she unpacked. If only she had music playing in the cabin to cover the noise. Instead, she flipped on the sink faucet, and then used the toilet. Upon flushing, the darn thing sounded like a noisy vacuum. She grimaced and dumped out the necessities to revive her face. No way would he not have heard that racket.

Wash, tone, lotion were automatic, like setting an alarm for work. She shut off the water. A quick application of brown eyeshadow and black liner required precision to draw out the almond shape of her eyes. Blush was a random, slap-dash thing for her. The berry-blast lipstick, however, had to be perfect and applied with care because she had cupid lips. Little peaks, directly under the bridge of her nose, had to be outlined or she'd have big red clown lips instead of little rosebuds. In addition, her bottom lip was bruised, so her usual gnawing hurt. She bent in half and brushed her hair. Upright again, she added a cloth coated rubber band, loosely knotted the hair at her nape and added another fastener to keep the curls in place.

Finished, she opened the door to find John sitting on the sofa, one leg braced on the other and an info flyer--apparently about the ship as *Verbena Skylark* was splashed across the first page--open on his lap.

He lifted his head. His eyelids went half-mast.

Her heart caught again. Maybe she was coming down with something. Lust came to mind. Could he be a potential donor after all?

"I liked your hair down better." His gaze was hot, heating her even more. With a single flip, the magazine closed and fell onto the tiny coffee table.

She stepped off the platform and as graceful as a ballet dancer, swayed toward him. "Thanks."

She sat beside him on the tiny sofa, which put their thighs together. Hormones raged, jetting pulsations to her lower region. Her clit tingled. "My friends insisted I come on this cruise to get over a love affair gone wrong. They encouraged me to meet a load of hot, nice guys."

"I think that's what single's cruises are designed to do." Poker face looked good on him.

She couldn't mention the donor project because a woman looking for a baby-daddy was a sensitive issue. Men got all quirky about legalities, financial responsibilities, and even if she had no interest in the man participating in the raising of the child, the guy, if he was high on the donor list of prospects, might feel a need to be involved. Which was why she'd jumped into treatment after Conrad said yes. He'd been okay with the prospect of being a detached father. Of course, she hadn't known at the time he'd be buying a vacation home with stolen diamonds while she might be rotting in jail.

"I thought maybe we could work together to filter out the people we don't want to be with."

"Okay, I'm in research, so I understand your reason to sort information, evaluate your data, and select possible dating material." He talked like a math person. Statistical analysis was her weak point for sure. "What do you have planned?"

Hot cheeks, raging clit--she had to get cool. Pitch the idea and go get a drink. "Well, I thought we could help each other. More than likely there are twice as many females on this ship as males--"

"Six thousand passengers and three thousand employees. Of the six K probably sixty-two point four percent are female."

She dropped her hands from pressing against her face. "Okay. So there are more women than men. What I propose is we cover for each other. If an undesirable approaches me, I'll turn him away by claiming we're together. You can do the same. At the end of the night, we'll select our chosen guy or girl and be on our merry way."

His gaze roamed over her face and focused on her eyes. "What if you're making a bad decision? Your data may be skewed by alcohol or slick magazine-cover good looks. Do I have the right to tell you?"

"Ah." She lifted an eyebrow. "How about we test the market and see what happens first?"

His almond shaped eyes widened. "What about a safe word?"

"Pardon?" She crossed her legs and flicked her fingernails.

"Let's say you've chosen your partner and later find out he's not what you thought. You could give a shout-out...ah... 'Bang Wang' and I'll come running."

"Bang Wang?" She held in the laughter and was very proud of herself for not even giving way to a smile.

Red appeared on his neck and cheeks. She must not have hid her expression after all. "I'm sorry. I think it's a perfect shout-out for help." She nodded.

"First thought that popped into my head," he said and looked at his shoes.

"We'll see how tonight goes and then decide. Although, I think you'll need one, if there is a significant difference in male and female guests. You're going to be hit on more than me. Toss around a few suggestions for a good code word when the cougars come after you." She tapped her chin with a finger.

"I won't need one." His hand dragged through his short dark hair.

"Oh, why won't you?"

"Because I've a hard shell and keen instincts when it comes to people." He stood, as if the topic made him nervous.

Diamonds were the hardest everlasting mineral on earth. All women wanted to enhance their beauty by the glittering glow of the sparkles. John would be superlative arm candy for any woman on the cruise. The perfect fit for him. "What do you think of *diamonds*?"

He jerked as if sucker-punched. "Diamonds?"

"Yes. They're the hardest jewel on earth, they sparkle and they're priceless. I'm thinking *diamonds* is the perfect code for you." She stood, tugged her vest, and walked around the coffee table. "Ready?"

"Yes, more than you know." He slowly rose from the sofa.

Chapter 3

John Kajiyama, Special Investigation Agent, wanted to go into his stateroom and immediately erase the interaction from his memory, and the tape before it got admitted into evidence. His colleagues at Atlantic Coast Investigations would tease him endlessly for the *Bang Wang* comment, if word ever got out. He knew without a doubt the bug he'd hidden while Mary was freshening-up would have caught his surprise at the mention of diamonds.

He shook his head as he followed Mary down the corridor. Bang Wang. His only excuse was her tempting body and quick wit, in addition to being on an adult cruise. She'd think any randy male passenger would hit on her, so he'd played the part. Yes, that's what he'd tell his colleagues when they were laughing their asses off. He was adapting to the role.

Would she take a *partner* back to her room each night? He'd have difficulty listening to the bump and grind, knowing she was with someone other than him. According to the patterns forming from the data on the pivot chart, Conrad Peabody would eventually contact her, maybe even on the ship or in one of the ports. One way or another he'd find out if she was part of the robbery.

John's associate, Debbie Gilbert, would also be searching for Peabody or his partner in crime, Andee Waterman, on the cruise. The thieves were caught on tape for a total of one minute and fifty nine seconds robbing Keefe's Finest Jewels, enough to show them using a gun and binding Mary's wrists and blindfolding her. Fortunately her sales clerk had gone to a dental appointment, which made Mary's role in the heist all the more suspicious.

Waterman had been the one to disable the guard and the camera. The close up indicated he had a tobacco chewing habit. When John and Debbie got past the yellow police tape and into the store, he'd secured a sample of the brown spit and sent the evidence to ACFI's lab. DNA led them to Waterman, who had priors. A simple match and evidence was logged. The two thieves had laid a clever escape route and immediately gone underground.

John's gut told him they would appear on the cruise or at one of the ports. Needless to say the passenger manifest didn't list their given names. Debbie had verified the employees on paper, and during the cruise she'd evaluate the crew with a great deal of care, looking for the two criminals.

Loud blasts of calypso music punctured his eardrums as Mary led him into the pool area. Merry makers were already sipping on straws coming out the top of fake coconut shells. Strong perfume scents rippled through the breeze blowing off the warm ocean water. Many of the colorful sarongs women were wearing wouldn't be enough material to keep them comfy when the wind took on a chill later in the night. But of course, that could be the very reason they wore the thin, short garments. This was hook-up central.

He had four days to discover if it had all been a con and Mary was in on the game. He'd attach to her like an insect to a fly strip.

She sidled up to the Tiki Station, a bar decorated in palm leaves, fake torches and curved banana-shaped bar stools. The bartender--Ryan according to his tag--offered Mary a tuberose and orchid lei. His hands slid along her breasts as he lowered the ring of flowers. Mary's bosom lifted and lowered as if she breathed excitedly. The floral scent filtered into John's nostrils. While he appreciated the simple beauty of the white, lavender and magenta necklace, he didn't like the interaction between Mary and Ryan.

Across from the Tiki Station, a reggae band ended a song by Bob Marley, and to John's surprise and pleasure, started *Right Time*, by The Mighty Diamonds. John took a seat beside Mary and held his palm out as Ryan offered him the lei. Too bad she didn't offer to lei him.

"Here." John held out the flowers. She winked and wrapped the delicate blooms around her wrist.

"Tonight's specials are the Mai Tai and the Zombie. Either of you interested?" Ryan held a Tiki mug, a square coconut with a face embossed on the side. The bartender was ready to create the magic of an island drink.

"What's in a Zombie?" She leaned on the bamboo surface and held her face cupped in her hands.

"Fruit juices, rum, apricot brandy, and a cherry," Ryan said.

"I'll take a Zombie," John answered and clicked on his Blackberry to read a text, but watched Mary.

Mary leaned farther on the counter and whispered into Ryan's ear. He grinned as if her closeness was an extreme tip. John had to agree. Her lips touching his ear would be well worth more than any cash reward.

"Orgeat syrup?"

She nodded.

"Okay then, one Zombie and one Mai Tai." Ryan set a tall glass and a coconut cup on the counter. Mary quizzed the guy about his family and life style. Was this job his living, as in life's goal, or just a break from existence?

Ryan didn't pause in his drink preparations as he answered her laundry list of questions. He was clearly interested in her as a woman, not just for the tips. John didn't listen to all of her questions, but what he did overhear made him curious about her odd interrogation. Maybe small talk wasn't part of her nature, as she told Ryan her aunt had provided the cruise and then passed away from a massive heart attack. As far as John knew, she'd told a lie. If she was trying find a method to sell the diamonds, her technique was weird and off course.

Ryan went into his family's history as he plopped the ugly brown mug, complete with a yellow umbrella, beside John. With a half-smile, he set a highball glass with an orchid and pineapple slice on the lip in front of Mary.

She took a sip. "Umm, this is good. I can taste the almonds and orange flower water. What did you call it?"

"Orgeat syrup, but it's not nearly as sweet as you, Mary." The beverage aficionado's voice was as sweet as the syrupy drink.

Her thirty-carat smile came into play, and despite the pleasant buzz from the Zombie, John wanted to barf. He swiveled around to evaluate the other passengers and the staff, hoping to spot Waterman or Peabody and get this gig over with before he made more of a fool of himself. Some couples danced in the taped-off area near the pool, but many women simply stood, swaying to the music. A few glanced his way, so he nodded in acknowledgment.

Mary dug through her large handbag and drew out her phone. A moment later, she lined up a shot. John glanced at Ryan, who had no problem posing, and then rolled his eyes.

What Goes Around Comes Around jived from the three member band as a tall gangly blond man approached Mary from the back.

The thin guy swallowed and his Adam's apple, the size of a small Washington, moved up and down in his throat. "May I have this dance?"

Mary glanced at John. He shrugged. Her gaze shifted to the bartender, but he'd moved to the other end. "Sure, I'd like to dance."

She let him take her arm and lead her to the other side of the pool. Her movements were like her personality, varied, expressive and interesting. A slow version of *Have Mercy* by The Mighty Diamonds started and Adam's apple guy took her loosely into his arms. A gentle sway of her hips, although not touching his, drew many glances from the men at the bar. The rhythm of the music in conjunction with the ship's movement showcased her in a lazy, seductive mode. Man was made to suffer as the lyrics indicated, and without exception, John's jeans tightened at his crotch. He felt like a teen with his first Playboy. He had to get control over his physiological impulses.

Her wrists and arms were exceptionally well defined. As a jewelry designer, she used her muscles: arms, wrists and fingers, but John wouldn't have noticed until she raised her beautiful limbs into the air, tracing graceful movements with her hands.

"Christ," he muttered, and without looking reached to the side and clutched his drink. A sip proved the beverage was Mary's, surprising him. The rum was missing--she was drinking a virgin Mai Tai. Why would she go to a bar, pretend to be drinking, but chose not to imbibe? Maybe she wanted to be in control, minimize the chance she could let information slip about the heist to anyone. The lady was a mystery, and he would thoroughly enjoy unfolding her secrets and making all of the amalgams come together.

"Hi, my name's Wanda," a woman said, titillating his ear drums with her sultry voice.

He glanced at her bleached-blond, piled high hair, tan circa 1980 and spandex top that barely covered her solid breasts. Yeah, right. Not in a million years, even if he were desperate.

"John." He nodded and turned his focus to Mary. The band ended the song.

Wanda's skirt slid noisily together as she leaned. Her gaudy red mouth touched his ear. "I'm very wicked, if you know what I mean."

John wasn't taking his gaze from Mary as her hips swayed in time to the music. She strode toward him. Her eyes sparkled as she drew closer and reached around his back to snag her liquor free drink.

"I see you've a new friend." She held out her free hand. "Mary."

"Wanda," she stage whispered into John's ear and resituated on the stool. Her skirt rode up her thighs to a nearly obscene level as she crossed her legs. Her smile matched the monkey face on the tiki bar pole. She held aloft a shot glass filled with brown liquid.

Mary dropped her arm and placed her drink on a cocktail napkin on the bamboo bar.

"Diamonds," John hissed.

"What'd you say?" Wanda shouted.

A snort, loud enough to be heard over the drums, came from Mary before she wrapped her arm around his shoulder. Her purse bumped against his back. She kissed the side of his lips and slipped her hand under his polo. "Wanda, sorry, but John's my guy, and I don't share."

In the moment, John closed his eyes to readjust and get his control back. His heart snapped against his rib cage, adding to his lust misery.

Adam's apple said, "Mary, here you go, Zombie, just for you."

"Oh, Kyle, I'm sorry, but I'm exhausted so I'm heading out. Here, Wanda, a fresh Zombie, and I'd like you to meet Kyle. He's a self-made merchandizing millionaire. His story is sooo fascinating."

John jumped off the stool and swiveled it around for Kyle to sit. Two seconds later, John had Mary's wrist, tugging her toward the exit. A glance proved Wanda's hands were testing the merchandise. The musicians sang Marley's *No Woman, No Cry*.

"Don't worry, John, everything's going to be all right," Mary sang in a Jamaican accent.

His pulse pounded as hard as the waves beating the side of the ship, and arousal spiraled through him, flushing his skin with heat.

Arms entwined, they strolled into the hallway. A group waited at the elevator for the doors to open. His throat dried, he couldn't swallow. Was she planning on going to another bar? Age had caught up with him; almost forty was too old to chase after a twenty-nine-year-old bombshell. Not for the first time in the past hour, he wished for his sweet unobtrusive data-gathering desk job.

"How old are you, John?"

Could she read his thoughts? "Thirty-nine."

"So you got hit on by your first cougar." The corridor was blessedly quiet the farther away from the pool they got. "I didn't think they'd migrate down from the Forever Lounge on the bow of the twelfth deck this early in the cruise." The ding of the elevator arriving disrupted the silence.

"Hardly hit on by a cougar, since I'm not a teen. Do you know where all of the bars are located?"

"Yes, thanks to my friend, Jenn." Mary stood in front of the elevators, but got her key card out of her bag and slid a glance at her watch.

"She designed the ship?" He shifted to her other side, as if to continue down the hallway.

"No, but she wanted me to know where all the hot spots were. You'll need to go to Forever and search for a chick. All of the young ones will be hunting on that ground." She walked backward. "Night, John."

Wait!

She turned and sashayed down the corridor. The elevator doors whooshed open and chatty women in colorful loungewear exited. He shook his head and entered the lift. Mary appeared to be going to her room. His recording device would capture her interactions, so he'd search for the escaped thieves.

John closed his eyes. Would the Tiki bartender's shouts of ecstasy be taped tonight?

Chapter 4

Mary scratched the top of her right foot with her left big toe. The bright red nail polish matched her bikini perfectly. She'd considered adding a toe ring, but not wanting a tan line on one of her toes, declined. The Wave Pool was empty except for a couple of children with their mother. Large sunglasses hid the woman's eyes, but she acted tired, like she needed a vacation from her vacation. Although designed around adults, children were on the cruise. It was a chance for families to relax together and reconnect, she supposed.

"Do you have photographs of your sister?" Mary gazed at First Mate Matthew Taylor. He fit all of her categories perfectly. All she needed to do was see one of his relatives for a DNA scan of sorts. Matthew's knee rubbed against her oil-slick thigh as he perched on the edge of the lounge chair next to hers. His dirty blond hair and longish nose didn't bother her in the least. He was athletic and the way his white uniform fit proved he hadn't exaggerated when he'd described his workout routine.

"I wish I did," he said. "Up for a run in a couple hours? It's two miles around the decks, and I'll show you the bridge." He winked, grinning. His eyes were an amber color, not brown, not yellowish, but more of a dark muted orange. Good-looking and husky voiced, he drew her gaze every time he opened his mouth.

One of the wayward children screamed a long, piercing wail, drawing their attention to the trio again. A boy had fallen and held his knee in his shaking hands. Even from a distance his little lips could be seen quivering.

"I'll be back." Matthew took off running, rounding the curve of the pool deck like a seasoned sailor. As he gently administered care to the youngster, the mother hovered and the little girl clung to her mother's black and white striped sarong.

Mary's stomach tingled in excitement. He was perfect, and obviously loved kids, as evidenced by his relaxed body motions and soothing tones that carried in the wind. She withdrew her notebook and added the details before she forgot. Matthew Taylor, DNA: perfect in structure, no odd body growths. A sister going into an art program. Organs were in good shape, tight runner's muscles and rarely, if ever, drank alcohol. Never smoked. Nice, easy going and especially thoughtful, as he told her he'd be right back. Outstanding looks, 'nough said. Was he resourceful? Intelligence would be important in offspring.

Covering a yawn, she glanced at Matthew. He was wrapping a white cruise towel around the child's knee, then cradled the boy and carried him to the elevator. Matthew turned and nodded to her. He'd be back. Yes, he was resourceful and honorable. The wind blew the page over, so she continued writing accolades for her number one pick.

"Donor. What does that mean?" John slipped onto the lounge next to her.

"It's my list to help me narrow the search for a prospective suitor."

He didn't look wrung-out, so he must have gotten some sleep.

Mary hadn't gone directly to bed because of the surprise she'd found in one of her fashionable, trendy high heels. A bag of uncut diamonds wedged in the toe. She'd spent most of the night sewing stolen diamonds onto her evening bag. The process to remove the agate stones and place the diamonds in the clasp had been long and intense. Her tiny nail kit and borrowed silverware made the task cumbersome and time consuming. Conrad must have intended to go on the cruise, and if the luggage hadn't made it through the scanner, she would have gone to jail.

At five bells, she'd crawled into bed and slept like an innocent. She should turn in the jewels at the next port. But, what if...

"You know this pool is at the bow, on top level, and will be very rocky if we hit waves." John lay against the stretchy fabric of the seat and closed his eyes.

"Yep. I've found I don't get motion sickness, which is odd because I sit all day at work, so I don't have a resistance built up or anything." Notes finished, she glanced at the entry. Damn, she hadn't taken a photo. Matt would come back, and she'd take one then. She set her phone on the table as a reminder. "Did you have a good time last night?"

"Yes. Very interesting." His reply didn't satisfy her curiosity. "What do you do? Your profession?"

"I'm a jewelry designer. Did you meet some fascinating babes at Forever?" Why was she so curious?

"Um hum, danced under the stars. Beautiful and enjoyable. You should have been there." The binding on the chair creaked as he leaned forward. In a flash, his shirt came off and he tossed it on the table with her phone.

Her breath caught in her throat. Last night she'd touched his hard muscles covered in smooth skin, and today she got to see them. He was spread eagled against the chair, and his sculpted, hairless chest drew her attention. A six-pack wasn't evident, and he did have a couple of tiny egg rolls on the sides, but all in all, John Wang was sexy adorable.

"Why are you up here? I thought you wanted to search for the perfect partner." His shoulders lifted and lowered on the lounge as he settled. He kicked off his sandals. Even his toes were hairless.

"Because of the waves, they provide a nice little foreplay." She threw out the bait, knowing it would catch any single guy's attention, as she withdrew a novel from the bag. Excitement skittered through her stomach, but she resisted smiling and pointed her focus on John's face.

"Okay, I'll bite." He lifted his sunglasses, his brown-eyed glance probing.

"This pool is one of the most popular because of the motion. As you're swimming laps, a jarring will occur and you'll literally float over the person next to you." She winked. "The stronger the wave, the greater the friction. I imagine more than sun tan oil is lubricating this pool."

"I doubt that. Probability is--"

"Only one way to find out." One sandal hit the deck and she tried to toe off the other one.

"Anything to get you out of that overly large garment," he muttered.

She slid the crimson and white orchid-printed robe from her shoulders. The tiny little bikini she'd just been able to wiggle into flashed in the early sun. Blood red and held together by thin gold snaps on each hip and between the breasts, she'd purchased the scrap of nothing with sex on her mind. Albeit she'd intended to only have intercourse with her lover of the past year, but life was ever changing and she'd roll with the waves.

"Put it back on." John held the cover-up in front of her.

"Silly, we can't swim if I'm weighted down." She looked for the stairs. "Come on, it's early enough we won't have a lot of strangers getting on our stuff."

She took a couple of steps forward and dived, shoved off the bottom and quickly came to the surface. Cold. Cold water. She flung hair away from her face and looked around. Where was John? Like a seal in the Atlantic, he swam beside her, dragging his hands along her legs.

His arms held steady at the sides of her breasts. The narrow string was hardly a barrier.

Mary's hands went beneath his cold-pimpled nipples and together they paddled, staying afloat. "I can tell you're a good swimmer."

"Maybe I'm just good at holding my breath?"

She shook her head. "No, I didn't hear a splash and you glided through the water."

He had rhythm and a part of her wanted to be into him, because she imagined he was also very good at the baby-making thing.

"Are you asking me to race?" He tilted his head to one side to dislodge water.

"Not now that I know you're an Olympian. How about one freestyle lap down and back just to prove my point?" His hands hadn't moved and the frigid water made her nipples peak. Their connection felt awkward and comfortable at the same time.

His beautiful mouth formed a lopsided smile. Did he know what he did to her? "You think one lap is enough foreplay?" Finally he lifted a set of five and stroked the side of her face. "Not enough for me. I require a little build up before I blow the load."

"From what I heard, you'll get all that you wish from the gyrations." With a flourish, she held out her arm. Sprinkles of water glittered in the early morning sunrays. "Shall we?"

He laughed and eased onto the surface. "Ladies first, and I guarantee my woman will always be the first to come."

Flapping her feet to keep upright, she flipped onto her back. She hoped what Jenn's friend Stubbing had told her about the Wave Pool was accurate. Hormones had her frazzled. Her vagina was already tightening in eager anticipation.

John's strong strokes, in the American crawl, took him a few meters away. The guy was a competitor. She backstroked and could tell from the markers on the side walls they were near the end. Not one wave pounded them. Damn, she hated to be wrong.

As she flung her right arm out, the water moved. A slow rise at first, and then a great force like being on a paddle-boat in the center of a hurricane. John held strong, but at the second wave he landed on top of her. Grabbing the edge of the pool, he held them together and locked in place as another current hit them broadside. She went under and panic set in, her heart pounded in her ears and her breath caught. Frantic, she blew out air and anxiously clutched for the surface. John's hand went around her wrist and dragged her until she was wedged between him and the pool's handrail.

All of her body parts touched his. He kept them connected until the liquid leveled. Security surrounded her, providing her with a sense of safety for the first time in several weeks.

Mary wiped the chlorine-scented water from her face and tried to catch her breath. John wasn't breathing heavy at all. They were so snug; her nipples had to be piercing his chest.

"Your heart's racing," he whispered into her ear.

A whistle spouted sharp tones.

"That was a rush, wasn't it? Guess it got me aroused." Aggressiveness wasn't part of her nature, but he created a fire in her. A strange fear that only he could satisfy the tingling building in her lower region made her want to move, to flee.

Until he nuzzled her neck, then her thoughts scattered and her clit clutched with need. "What?"

The man wasn't anywhere near her donor choice, but he sparked her to life. She hadn't felt this exhilarated since...ever. He was kind, funny, sexy, and most of all, if his necking was a prelude, John would be a world class kisser. She had to stop him. Candidate number one would be returning any minute. She bowed her head, focused on what lay beneath the water. "Heart's beating fast because I'm hormonal and you know what effect cold has on a woman."

John jumped back fast, creating a whirlpool. "Maybe we should return and get warm."

His tone was as chilled as the water. He flipped like a sea lion and snapped his arms in the stream as if racing time. Mary took a deep breath and used the strength of her legs to catch him. A second wave rolled her over him and she bottomed. The strong surge sent him several meters in front of her.

He stopped and looked at her as if he was trying to calculate the odds. She must have stirred his interest, because he flung out his fingers to reach for her.

She clung to her human life preserver, and he tugged her to his side. Together they drifted to the end. Mojo or not, the man had chivalry way down deep in his bones and she fell a little more in like with him.

His palm fit nicely on her rear as he hoisted her onto the edge of the pool. Breathing heavily, she shivered. Not enough sun to warm the skin. A white towel appeared before her. She looked up.

Matthew grinned at her and presented her with the ray of sunshine she needed, then held out a hand and pulled her to her feet.

"Thanks. That's very cold water in the morning." She held on tight.

"Here, John, take my towel." She dropped the thick cloth onto his lap and pivoted to sway with the motion of the ship to her lounge chair. After a purposely graceful sit, she lifted her finely turned legs onto the bench. To reduce stress, for the last two months, she'd been jogging, which had brought them into excellent form and deserving attention. She stretched and placed her arms behind her head. "I'm a naturalist. The sun will dry my skin."

John plopped onto the bench, shaking the metal feet in the process and coughed as if he were an orator preparing to lecture.

Matthew knelt beside her, stroked the edge of her hand. "I have to log some hours, but I'll see you around one. We'll take the jog around the perimeter?"

"Looking forward to it." She licked her lips, getting the chlorinated water from the surface, and then reached for her phone, needing to get a photo.

His focus remained on her mouth, the peaks, if she were to guess. The cupid's bow always drew interest. "Umm, me too."

"First Mate Taylor, you're to report to the bridge." A man's deep voice resonated among the pipes decorating the top deck, where speakers had been cleverly camouflaged. The pool was nice, but it was surrounded by huge white cylinders, hiding people and spouting loud noises much of the time.

The announcement provided her an opportunity to get a shot of Matthew as he stood.

"I'll see you later." He winked and touched her skin again, above the knee, not quite on the inner thigh. Donor number one took off at a brisk pace.

John hadn't said two words since the wave pool. She bent to put the phone in her bag, while trying to come up with a conversation starter. Upright again, he frowned, which made her reconsider. Maybe the comment had made him angry. Had he misunderstood her and thought she referred to the deflating effect chilled water had on men? Heat rushed to her face. Fact was, men's penises did shrink in the cold and women's nipples peaked, but she wasn't bold enough to discuss the male anatomy.

"I saw you dancing last night. You're very rhythmatic," a guy said, his voice lifting at the end as if air was difficult to obtain.

Mary drew her attention from John and glanced at the speaker. Body builder, sun worshiper, thick neck, squinted blue eyes and one of his eye teeth crossed over the tooth in front of it. What a list. Was rhythmatic a word?

"Thanks. I'm Mary." She smiled, but didn't hold out her hand.

"Billy Martinson, 2009 winner of Verona Beach Body Building Contest." He held his right arm in a typical muscle-man pose, exhibiting all the bulges in his upper bicep. Granted, he looked mighty fine, but she wanted brains, not a tight body. Of course, both would be a plus.

"That's nice, Billy. Is that your occupation, body building?" She itched to get her notebook out. All research should contain both positive and negative values.

"Naw. I work at a tool and die in Verona. Ten years now."

Yep, his hands had telltale burns or cuts from the machinery. Maybe he was paying his way through school.

"Interesting. I'm a Certified Bench Master Jewelry Designer, studied at the Charleston Jewelry Design Institute in South Carolina." The gold latch on the side of her bathing suit bit into her side. She should snap it and get her back-up guy's attention.

Billy, already on the edge of the lounge next to her, scooted the chair closer. He rubbed a finger across her hand and trailed the digits along her arm. "My studies are taken from life. I don't need to get more book learnin'."

Bile rose to her throat at his touch. Reaching for the suntan lotion in her bag, she met John's gaze. He smiled a wicked little knowing grin. If only she could stick out her tongue in a childish way.

"I was wondering if you and I could take a swim, play a little in the waves." Billy stood, providing her with his side view. The very tight blue spandex did nothing to hide his endowment. No amount of cold water would deflate that.

She shot her gaze to John. He winked, nodded toward the pool, and closed his eyes again.

"I'm sorry, Billy, but I promised First Mate Taylor I'd run laps with him in about an hour, so I'm going to have to get a little food in order to keep pace." Wickedness rolled through her as fast as the waves in the pool. "John's quite the swimmer, if you want a race."

John's eyes shot open, and his pupils dilated to be the size of Morgan Dollars, extra-large in their almond casings.

Mary shoved her sunglasses, diary, and sarong into the bag. Sandals on, she said, "See you later."

"Wait, I'll join you," Billy shouted, drawing the attention of a new group of wave riders coming on deck.

"No, thank you. Bye." She wove through the group of women, keeping hidden as much as possible, bypassed the elevator and ran down the stairs.

Her empty stomach gnawed. Holding the bag between her knees, she wrapped the cover-up around her. A quick glance in the glass case holding a fire extinguisher showed her hair was separating into chunks. She snagged a large toothed comb and a cloth-coated tie from inside the carry-all. As she raked her hair into some sort of order, she came to the conclusion she needed a haircut. Not just trimming off the splits, but a style, rather different, something to change her appearance and maybe hide her from Conrad. Now that she'd found where he'd stashed the diamonds, she guessed there was a ninety-nine percent probability he would stop at nothing to find her. She looped the sea air blown strands of hair into a knot and twisted the elastic band to hold the tail in place. He wouldn't get her. She'd fight 'til the death.

Chapter 5

"You're getting a tan?" Debbie, dressed in a black slip of nothing, settled onto the lounge chair Mary had vacated. Before the trip, John had voiced his desire to avoid the sun. His normal skin tone was the color of light maple, but a few days under the rays, and his hide changed to raw umber.

"Thought I'd dry out before I go below deck. How's it going?" John spotted a blonde, resembling Mary in every way except for the tight rear, riding the waves along with a balding thirty-something. Mary's bum and her naturally large breasts had a little more jiggle.

"Nothing so far." Resting firm against the blue and white striped cushions, Debbie closed her eyes. Her auburn hair had been washed, dried and styled to perfection. Finger and toe nails were all faultlessly pumiced and painted. She was a diva, but also reported to be the best field agent with Atlantic Coast Investigations. Her FBI field experience made her especially valuable.

John leaned over the side of the lounge, pretended to pick up his phone and whispered, "After this case, I'm going back to my desk job."

He wanted nothing more than to be at his small cubical right now instead of having his convoluted emotions tethered to Mary.

A chuckle slid from low in Debbie's throat. He imagined the sexy sound had gotten her a lot of dates at headquarters. "Then I guess we'll be parting ways, because I love being in the field investigating fraud. Most of the time I get restaurant fires, which doesn't give me the opportunity for undercover work. We're a perfect fit, and I'm glad they asked us to take this assignment."

Screams and laughter came from the pool. John glanced at the partiers getting their ride-on. An opportunity to get close to Mary, find out more about her as a person and possibly discover where the diamonds were hidden, had fallen right into his lap. He wasn't certain if she even knew the jewels' location, but Mary was smart, and as such she'd stash them somewhere. Her possible involvement in the heist continued to weigh heavy.

Playing tag with the criminal activity scenario was the memory of how her body responded to his. The distance between them had burned away, their beings fused. He'd kissed her neck, experienced her pulse rate increasing as his lips touched her wet skin. His cock had danced as he'd sniffed her chorine and coconut scented body pressing into him, spiking high as the waves in the pool. That was until she made the nasty remark about the cold. All men's dicks shrink in artic temperatures and his had lost the happy momentum. Was she trying to repel him? Did she know he was a detective? Christ. He rubbed his chest as heartburn, sudden and sharp, infiltrated the space.

What was she searching for on this cruise? Why would she have taken the trip so soon after the jewelry store robbery? Maybe she was hoping to connect with her ex and his partner. Worst case scenario for him, she was trying to find a buyer for the diamonds at one of the ports. Could the vacation be a decoy to throw the cops and insurance investigators off?

So far she'd only been attracted to workers on the ship. What about the single passengers? Granted, the two who'd approached her were bargain basement rejects, but if her goal was as she'd stated to find a mate, then wouldn't she look beyond someone who was tied to a ship traveling all the time? Mary Keefe's actions didn't match her words, and John believed direct dealings with individuals told more of the truth than expressions any day. He trusted in logical sequences and facts. None of the data added up.

"I'm going to get a bite and see if I can cruise through the kitchen. The staff remained hidden most of the time during my questioning, so I'll need to find a way in." Debbie slid her long legs off the side of the lounge.

Her double D's came close to his face as she whispered, "Don't get involved with your suspect, Kajiyama!"

Not even her silicone based orbs brought him to life. Maybe this assignment had made him a eunuch. No, the icy water had indeed deflated him, because his cock had filled and lifted when Mary shed her blanket and exposed her luscious breasts, perfectly formed belly button and delicate ankles. In addition, he'd had no difficulty getting it up when she landed on him yesterday.

"I'll go with you. I'm hungry, and I like to see you in action." He slipped into his sandals and stood.

She grinned. "You like to see people scurrying around at my commands?"

"Yeah, I envision you as a..." He'd completed sensitivity training and could not finish his thought without violating the rules. Hopefully the interruption seemed natural as he tugged on his shirt.

"Dominatrix?" She laughed. "You'll wonder now if I have the outfit to match the attitude, won't you?"

Heat rushed to his face, so he wiped his face with a hand towel. His thoughts had gone in that direction. Yep, he wasn't a eunuch after all.

"Can't hide behind the dark cloth, John, I know the red isn't from the sun." She picked up a cotton satchel with palm leaves spread across the surface and rifled through it until she drew a silky gray fluff from inside.

"Hey, if you're leaving, can we have your lounges?" the blonde he'd watch play in the waves asked. She dripped water onto the porous surface, shedding the liquid from her body as a snake would its skin.

"Sure." John gathered his magazine, green striped towel, Blackberry and oil.

As the boisterous passengers took their seats, John escorted Debbie to the elevator.

A quick ride down, and they arrived at the dining hall. John wrapped his arm around Debbie's waist as they passed a group of happy vacationers. The door to the dining hall was massive and lined in teak, the brown wood appearing so soft, yet he knew it was rock hard. Various scents of pungent onions, grilled meat and sweets wafted under his nostrils.

They stepped across the threshold. Mary stood in front of him, ready to slip past. The clatter of china and crystal didn't override the beat of his heart at the simple sight of her star-studded beauty. When had he started thinking in cosmic poetry?

Her eyes widened as she moved closer. Why did he continually get the impression she could read his mind?

"I guess you found a new friend," she whispered into his ear, shocking his internals into battling for more of her. She shifted her focus to Debbie and flung out a hand. "Hi, I'm Mary."

"Debbie Becker." She took Mary's hand, while bumping her hip against his. A quick shake, and Debbie glanced from Mary to him. "Isn't he the cutest?"

"Oh, yeah, he's adorable," Mary replied. Her tone had a snap. She held up her hand, a slip of white paper between her fingers, and waved. "I'll let you get to your lunch. Have fun."

"Sounds like your girlfriend's jealous," Debbie said.

John kept his gaze on Mary's cute rear as she traipsed out of the room. Debbie tugged his arm, toward a table near the buffet. There was a multitude of food choices. However, he seemed to have lost his appetite. Was Mary heading off to her room to give the sailor a test run? Visions of her naked, squirming around on the bed, trying to get satisfaction made his gut clench. Her future boyfriend was right next door. She should only be with him.

"At least get some fruit." Debbie's plate was piled high with a variety of shellfish and bread. How she could eat all of that and remain thin baffled him.

Items stowed on the spare seat, John dragged a ceramic plate from the stack and threw an odd mix of vegetables and fruit onto the surface.

By this time a good majority of people were in the dining room. John's focus remained on Mary's possible mattress workout. His conversation with Debbie became limited to weather, the first port stop and their plans for the evening. With three-fourths of her food gone, Debbie dug through her bag and pulled out a badge.

She grabbed the attention of the nearest server with a finger wave.

"May I help you?" The tiny associate would soon lose her sunny smile.

Debbie flashed her badge. "I'm with Food & Drug. Your shellfish was below the required temperature. I'll need to go into the kitchen and talk with your personnel."

The poor little girl kept her smile, but her hands were shaking as she pointed to the galley a few steps away.

"Coming, John?" Debbie asked as she stuffed her insurance investigator's badge into her bag.

"Yes, I'll scout the area while you're badgering the chef." John threw his napkin near the plate of uneaten food, stood, and gathered his sunglasses, phone and beach towel.

Inside the kitchen, Debbie talked as if she knew all the food and drug requirements for serving. The cook was amiable, although a muscle twitched in his jaw. John couldn't tell if Chef Pierre's face was red with anger or as a result of being surrounded by heat sources.

John drew Conrad Peabody's image to his cellphone screen and asked a couple of the talkative assistants hanging near the pots and pans if they'd seen him. The pastry chef claimed she'd danced with the guy a couple of nights ago before the new guests arrived, but he looked different. The man she'd shaken her groove thing with had black dreadlocks, dark eyes and a beard.

John joined Debbie as she completed her reminders of food safety, and they exited the kitchen, leaving the strong odors of cookies and fish frying behind them.

"Will you come with me to my room? I want to show you a portion of the robbery video." John selected the Up button on the elevator panel.

"Sure." Her dangling silver crescent moon earrings jingled as she flipped a lock of red hair behind her ear.

They entered the lift and stopped at the eighth deck level. Not one other person had entered as they rode. "Do you know what donor means in slang, or what it might be an acronym for?"

As Debbie listed her thoughts of what donor could represent, elements he'd already concluded were not possibilities, John tuned her out and thought of Mary. An hour had passed. If she'd had an afternoon fuck with the officer and gentleman, then they'd be done and he wouldn't have to endure thinking of her being in the next room with someone else.

Mary's surprise at seeing him with Debbie had been straightforward. Debbie was very attractive, not to him, but most of the men on the fifth floor of their building seemed to be engrossed with her appearance. John recalled Mary's facial expression as she'd whispered to him earlier. Although she'd said "friend," her eyes had been cold. No, *fuming* would be a better description. Could his little Mary truly be jealous, as Debbie said?

How could he test that theory?

His subject was walking down the hallway.

John grabbed Debbie and tossed her against the door. A smile, as wicked as he'd ever seen, spread wide on her perfectly made-up face. "Go along with me," he whispered.

Pressing her hands above her head, flat alongside the portal, he kissed her. Not a gentle, *thanks for the nice time* smooch, either. He added all the passion he'd built while following his little suspect-tease around the ship.

His obsession coughed. He could smell Mary over the cloying odor of Debbie's cologne.

Debbie separated her legs and nudged his knee to fit between her thighs, but his focus remained on the woman who'd smashed into his heart. Sweet Virgin Mary.

"Excuse me. I hate to interrupt, but could you move one door north of here?" Leg braced, she fluttered her delicate hands in front of her.

Her eyes were filled with fire. Debbie slid tighter onto his leg. She moved to the left and the knob of his knee slipped between the junction of her thighs. Repulsed at the action, he released Debbie and pulled her away from the entrance. "Sorry, didn't notice."

Mary grimaced. "Hey, if you're available at six, you and I have been invited to join the captain at the main table." She nodded at Debbie. "Sorry, only John and me."

"Sounds like something important. I'll pick you up at five forty-five." He smiled and wrapped his arm around Debbie's waist.

Debbie licked her ruby lips and moaned. "Plenty of time."

"Wonderful. I'll meet you at six." Mary slid her keycard into the slot and the door handle clicked. "Well, have fun."

Her tone level was as chilled as the shrimp should have been on the buffet.

"Shit, Kajiyama, it looks like she's really into you, too." Debbie tugged at her bathing suit top. "What did you want to show me? Hopefully more than your skills at tongue tango." She winked while flicking her tongue.

Swallowing the lump in his throat, he stared at the closed door. "Yes. All I needed was accomplished in sixty seconds or less." A shake of his head to get Mary out and to bring the case into focus didn't work. "I'll send you a clip of the video. Look at Waterman's body posture and movements. I wonder if he's transsexual."

* * * *

Mary fell against the door. Her breath caught as if she were an asthmatic like Lisa. Mary lowered her bag and clutched her chest. John wasn't her type, so why did seeing him kiss that redhead feel like sharp hot tweezers were being pressed into her lungs?

She dragged her feet forward and collapsed on the small bed. Placing the backs of her hands on her forehead, she contemplated her options. Two viable donor candidates were staff members here. She didn't know if they'd even engage in sex with guests. To get away from chatting with no-neck at the pool, she'd gone to eat. She was hungry, so the excuse had been valid. Matthew had sent her a note in the dining hall stating he couldn't meet her for a jog, but invited her and her friend, John, to join him at the Captain's Table for dinner. Matthew could be a doable candidate. But what about love? Would she be able to freely have unprotected sex with someone to whom she didn't have at least a smidgen of attachment?

Just to pad her selection a little more with intellectuals, she went to the library to see what single passengers might be interested in literature. As predicted, women and men with thick lenses and shirts buttoned to the top of their necks were reading there. They were easy to rule out, as the readers wouldn't tear away from the print to experience a night of passion. She'd have to go back to the pool or the Tiki Station later. Maybe John would be willing to join her at the bar, if she offered to buy him a Zombie.

John. Her heart clutched at the notion he'd found someone. Granted, Debbie had enough facial wrinkles to create a decent screen print, but he'd appeared to be getting his groove on.

Mary pounded her fists on the bed and then held her stomach as her muscles cramped. He wasn't her type. Then why did she want him? Why did seeing him kiss that woman make her heart ache? Were they next door, doing the shipboard mattress mambo?

Enough! Mary stood. She finger-combed her mass of kinks and snarls, then left the small cabin. A walk was what she needed. A stroll around the promenade, one lap, and then she'd get ready to woo Matt.

He was perfect for her. She clicked off the reasons why as she meandered around the pool and past the Tiki Station. The band members were setting their equipment out on the stage. She waded around the boxes. Stumbling a few steps, she tried to stand upright, but threw her hands out to catch herself if she landed on the concrete. A hand reached out and caught her before she landed on the hard surface.

"Watch your step," someone with a deep male voice said.

Mary straightened. Her stomach muscles gripped in pain.

Dark dreadlocks bounced off his shoulders as he hurried to help a band mate with a set of Calypso drums.

Conrad.

She resisted the urge to scream or call the ship's cops. Instead, she slowly rounded the corner and then picked up the pace. Her palms were sweating so much she couldn't get her room keycard to slide into the slot. She wiped her hands and tried again.

At the green light, she slipped inside and the keycard dropped in front of the closet as she wrapped her arms across her stomach. Sharp, wrenching pain ripped through her gut. Her friends were right. He was ruthless, and if he caught her alone, there was only one way she'd end up. Dead. Once he took the diamonds from her, she was a loose end that needed pinching off. She collapsed onto the brown sofa and rocked.

The first time she'd met Conrad, he'd sent flowers and candy, waited for her in the dark of the night so she wouldn't walk to her car alone. Tears dripped to her cheeks and fell onto her cover-up. They'd started dating. Six months later, knowing he wasn't the marrying kind, she'd proposed having a child together. He enthusiastically agreed. One miscarriage and several painful injections later, her uterus had been ready to accept sperm and develop a baby. The very day they were to conceive, Conrad set an explosive device on the secondary safe on the floor near the display cases and robbed her jewelry store.

He was an idiot, as her friends had claimed. A ski mask had covered his features, but he hadn't disguised his voice nor camouflaged his hand. He had a natural birthmark on his left thumb. In his right hand he'd held a gun. In plain sight the port wine-stain, shaped like an molar, beamed at her.

Mary threw herself flat on the couch. She scraped an escaping hair away from her face. Maybe she was mistaken. The police investigators said he was very clever to have made the bomb himself. She'd been used as an access point into the store and for him to scope out the vault. The insurance assessors had looked at her like she was guilty. Even her grandfather had interrogated her about the robbery. She'd reminded him that he'd approved Conrad as a suitor and possible father of Keefe heirs. Grandfather Keefe had pish-poshed and sent her home so he could finish closing the jewelry store for an indefinite period of time.

From the backside, dreadlocks didn't look like Conrad. Only his voice threw her into a tailspin. She'd never forget his pitch, low, sexy and distinct with a northeastern nasally intonation.

Enough deliberating. Either he was on the ship or not. Later, she'd visit the Tiki Station and get close to the reggae band. Lifting from the couch, she crossed to the closet and stood in front of the door. She exhaled, pulled the knob and removed the backpack purse. The scan machine hadn't caught anything odd about the items in her bag. White hot rage renewed inside her. Conrad had used her to carry the diamonds onboard. She almost wished the diamonds would have been sensed by the device and taken into custody, or that she'd missed the boat. Her heart thumped against her lungs. Danger wasn't something she was accustomed too. She had to stay cool and not panic.

She drew out the throw-away cellphone to check the battery. Solid bars appeared as she powered it, and then she quickly shut the mobile down. All was ready in case she needed to flee.

Chapter 6

Three light taps. John tuned into the chatter in the hallway, assuming Mary stood on the other side of the door. He threw the entrance open and glanced into the hallway. Estee Lauder perfume clouded the area, the same type his grandmother wore. A cougar was playing tricks. Then he heard the knocking again, a little harder this time and from the center of the room.

John flipped his laptop open and glanced at the screen. His investigation data and robbery video were on screen. He shoved the computer closed, drew his fake persona forward, and opened the between door. Derrick, his supervisor at ACI, had complained for a solid ten minutes about paying extra for the connecting rooms, but John had insisted. Instinct, from ten years as a detective on the Fort Meyers Police Force, gave him a keen sense of probabilities. He must stay near Mary in case she needed him when Peabody showed up. And he would, there was no doubt in John's mind. At the final draw he'd have to make a decision if she was guilty or innocent, based on proof.

She peered over his shoulder. "Are you alone?"

Her skin sparkled like star dust, smelling of chlorine mixed with a strong floral scent like the tropical gardens in his grandparents' home in Manoa, Hawaii, and he yearned to touch her. He had to experience the mix of the aromas and Mary herself. Stop. He needed to get his head back in the fraud investigation game.

"Yes." His voice came out like a croaky frog.

"I need help with this dress." She stepped over the threshold. Her high heels made her legs look impossibly long. His gut clenched. He had to gather control and maintain his role as investigator. No problem.

She pivoted.

No bra. Black thong. Hot. Possible diamond robbery suspect. He must ignore his urges.

"Ruby looks good on you. Draws out the natural peach tint to your skin." Could he sound any less male? He took a couple of steps to be in line with her narrow back. He blew a breath and held the two parts of the dress together and slowly zipped. Not wanting to get her delicate sun-kissed soft flesh caught in the teeth, he touched his fingers against the sweet channel of her spine as much as possible. Tiny sparkles glittered in the slight furrow of the small of her back. This activity was generally associated with partnered couples. His heartbeat quickened at the thought. "Did you forget the, ah, undergarment?"

"Nope. It's built in and uplifting." She twisted. "Want to see?"

Finished connecting the parts, he knuckled her forward. Deep inhale. Slow exhale. He was ready to see the final product. "Okay." The damn croak continued. Christ, what was wrong with him?

Her shoes were a nice focal point. With a hint of red on the soles, the height of the heels brought her level with his five feet ten inches. Hip hugging garment, which would account for the sexy thong. A heart-shaped bodice, with little pleats going from the valley disappearing under her arms. That was what he had to do to get through this, treat the little dressing session like a fashion show. He was an uninvolved spectator helping out. He quickly bypassed the bulk of skin flowing from the "uplifting" section, and all his good intentions fell away as he stared at her angel lips.

Her mouth had been outlined with a different, darker shade of her lipstick. The bruised bottom lip was nearly healed. Blush splattered across her cheekbones and strategic loose corkscrews of hair flowed on the sides of her face. Topping off the beautiful package were large square cut diamonds studs glinting from her earlobes. He hoped they were from the reputed Keefe family jewels instead of newly processed stolen stones.

"Nice earrings." Despite the sexy woman tantalizing him, he'd recaptured his normal, masculine tone. Too bad he couldn't talk about guy stuff instead of chatting on women's doo-dads.

"Thanks. You heard me tell no-neck that I'm a jewelry designer, right?"

"Yes." His mind jetted every which way as he tried to decide where she was going with the comment.

"Well, these little studs are not a sample of my work. They've been in the Keefe family for centuries." She caressed a fold in the dress with a finger. If only she'd stroke him like that. "Touch this material. What do you think?"

Little? They were probably a half-carat each. Touch the dress? Only if she wanted to lose the damn soft bit of nothing and have a go on the firm mattress a step away.

He stuck his fingers on her perfectly curved hip and then snapped them back.

"Electric shock?"

He shook his head, questioning what she meant. "What?"

"Your hand was there for like two seconds. Did you get shocked?" Her green eyes, all the more emerald because of the dark eye shadow, showed concern.

"Yes. A shock that's going to last a very long time."

She took a step back.

"Sorry. Are you ready to go?"

She hadn't caught his innuendo. He'd fallen for her, and once she was cleared of any suspicion, he planned to pursue a relationship, see if it could develop into something more. "Sure. Just need to straighten this tie."

"Here, let me help you." She pressed into him and whipped the knot out.

If logic ruled, instead of the lust currently ripping through his body, he should have refused and gotten as far away as possible from the hot situation. However, for the first time following a long string of relationships, he wanted her to return the emotion. He needed her to be in love with him. Love, he scoffed. He'd never used the word with a woman. After just a couple of days he was falling in love with Mary Keefe, jewelry designer slash socialite slash possible thief.

The *tap, tap, tap* of her palm on his chest matched his heartbeat. "What's wrong with you tonight? You're acting a little strange."

In reflex, he jerked away. "We've known each other less than two days. How can you possibly know if I'm acting strange or not?"

Pain crossed over her eyes, and she lowered her head as if to hide her thoughts. "I see."

He lifted her chin and gazed into her sweet face. "I guess I'm grumpy."

Her lips shot upward and a sparkle waved through her expressive eyes. "Didn't get any this afternoon?"

"Highly personal," he grumbled. "Ready to go? We'll be late."

"Just need to get my purse." She pivoted and swung her tight little ass through the opening.

He followed, leaving the two rooms adjoined.

* * * *

The guests occupying the Captain's round table were an odd mix. One Texas couple talked loud enough to be heard over the strings playing classical music in the background. Another couple, hailing from Minnesota, was quiet and focused on their food. A textbook salesman carried on an intense conversation with a librarian. Rounding out the group were perky blondes and a PR guy. A single man, a politician's public relations guru, had been seated beside Mary. His interest centered on John. Twenty agonizing minutes into the dinner, Mr. PR bowed his head near Mary's roasted chicken and touched her back as he chatted with Wang.

Mary wasn't sure what she'd expected, but she'd thought First Mate Matthew Taylor should have been glued to her side. With limited chances at conception, how could she entice the guy if he sat on the other side of a table setting of fourteen? One of the blond divas kept him occupied, but he stole a glance at her and winked. Dessert dishes were being placed and dinner plates removed. Port wine in a tiny glass added a deep purple color to the otherwise boring white arrangement.

John's hand brushed the side of her thigh as he lifted his napkin. All in all, the night had become tiring and painful to endure. Thoughts of dissecting the reggae band members made her stomach twist, but she had to resolve her suspicions. Her breath caught as she replayed the voice she'd heard a few hours ago.

For the second time, John's thick white cloth napkin fluttered to the floor directly under her gaze. Their heads banged as each reached for it. His fingers caressed the side of her face. Mary gazed into his penetrating eyes. What was he trying to convey? *Just say it.*

"Please get me away from here." He dropped his hand from her face and snagged the napkin. "Will you dance with me?"

"Heck yeah, when the captain releases us, we'll grind."

"Thank you!" He sounded so relieved she wanted to laugh, but considering she was at the Captain's table, she elected to hold the joy inside.

John's head popped up. Mary sighed, gathered control over her medicated raging hormones and lifted her upper body. Stomach muscles still fluttering as fast as the flag out the port window, she gave him a weak smile. Protocol was such they couldn't leave the table until the Captain dismissed them. Although she wasn't hungry, the dessert looked delicious, appearing to be a ball-shaped flan with swirls of white chocolate and caramel. Cute little twigs of dark coffee-tinted cookies were rising from the mound and spun sugar surrounded the tree-like accessory.

Fortunately, PR guy had diverted his attention to the poor woman on the other side of him. Mary was the first to be served, and until all the guests had plates in front of them she couldn't dive in.

"John, I'm going to use the restroom. I'll be right back," she whispered into his ear.

His almond eyes narrowed to be mere slits on his red-cheeked face. "You wouldn't leave me here?"

"No, I just need to, you know. I want to eat this fantastic dessert, and I promised to dance with you." She touched his protruding cheekbones to feel the heat. "You got a sun burn today. Want some lotion?"

His lips parted, but he appeared to have lost his voice. He shook his head.

Mary stood. The gentlemen at the table rose. She'd never been one to stand in the limelight and cursed her weak bladder for putting her there. Heat infiltrated her neck. She placed her napkin on the seat and grabbed her white glittery evening bag. A quick nod to Matthew and she hurried through the dining room, her cocktail dress swishing against her legs as she moved.

Women waited outside the ladies room, indicating the few stalls were full. Mary took a right and headed port side. Earlier she'd noticed a small restroom near the library. She opened the door to find it vacant, quickly locked it and took care of business. Hands washed, she unclasped her bag. Though she'd sewn the jewels hastily by hand, the beading looked quite nice. Not one person had made a comment about her rock-encrusted purse.

Reapplication of lipstick and a brush of mascara, and she was ready to finish dinner. Maybe Matthew would see her and John dancing and he'd interrupt. He'd take her into his arms and snuggle his tight body against hers. That sparkle in his eyes and bright smile got her heart to beat faster every time. Her nerve-endings would pulse and jump out of her skin if his cock pressed against her womanhood.

John. She couldn't ditch him. His touch created sparks. Maybe the electrical popping charged between them was a result of carpet static and not true emotion. Lust wasn't a simple emotion, it had existed from the time they'd fallen onto the sofa and continued as they'd been together almost every minute so far on the cruise. The adorable man grew on her like a rash. Granted, a very pretty red rash instead of something ugly, but a rash none-the-less. Like all surface abrasions, given time and treatment it would slowly disappear.

The corridor was quiet as she exited the restroom and trotted down the passage. She'd dance with John and then focus on Matthew. If he got called to work, she and John would hit the Tiki Station.

"Mary?" a man said in a deep, growling voice from the shadows.

Taken by surprise, she glanced down the passage. A dark figure moved closer to her, creeping like a ghoulish night animal. Long coiled hair sprung from under his knit hat. The safety lights mid-way down the hallway illuminated a glint of silver at the creature's side.

"Conrad," she squeaked.

Clutching her evening bag, Mary pivoted and ran. Heels clacking on the boardwalk, she rounded the edge. She grabbed hold of the wall to keep from sliding. In the next corridor, she could see a server carrying a large silver platter coming from an open door. Fortune prevailed, as she found the back entrance to the kitchen, behind the dining hall. A server had propped the portal ajar, while he took a smoking break. Yes, Lady Luck had smiled on her, and Mary took advantage, by slipping through the crack. As she followed a waiter carrying a laden tray of desserts, she regulated her breathing. The urge to glance around to see if Conrad remained on her heels was strong, but unadvisable. Her cover, a lost guest making her way to the dining room, wouldn't be valid if she kept peeking over her shoulder.

The double doors whooshed. At the sight of joyous partiers eating dessert, she'd made it to safety. Her tight neck muscles relaxed. She stuffed her purse under her arm and shook her fingers to bring life back into them as she wound her way to the Captain's table. The gents stood. John gave her a strange look, a mix of curiosity and concern, as he removed her napkin and pulled out her seat. Her lips moved into a half-smile. Most of her dinner mates had eaten their dessert. PR guy talked to his captive audience, she hoped keeping attention away from her. She placed her purse and then the cloth on her lap. Grabbing the port, she lifted it in salute to John and ungraciously drank the contents.

An alcohol rush zipped through her, making her slightly off-kilter. Throat burning, she sucked in air and placed the empty, small wine crystal on the table. She glanced at Matthew, who frowned and then directed his attention to ship-board Barbie.

No doubt, if Conrad caught her she'd be going overboard in the dark of the night. Pain ripped through her. Tomorrow, she'd have to escape and there wouldn't be a child for her. No one to have and to hold, to nurture, or provide a life filled with happiness. Childless, alone, and always running from the one who wanted to kill her had become her destiny. As she chased the wine with a deep drink of water, the Captain invited all of them to dance. The band strummed *Somewhere in the Night*.

John draped an arm across the back of her chair, touching her shoulder. "Try the sweet. You'll need the energy when I sweep you off your feet."

She snorted. Could she dance? Not having consumed alcohol for the past three months in preparation, the wine had gone straight to her head. The lights sparkled brighter and John looked dashing in his black suit and narrow necktie. The rust and cream swirls on the dark background came to vibrant life and drew attention to his strong, firm Matt Damon chin. Tie clutched in her hand, she dragged his handsome face close to hers. "I've lost my appetite for the concoction at the table."

His eyes widened, but that cute little grin appeared. He pried her fingers from his tie. "My place?"

"Only if you promise to dance with me," she whispered.

"Music style?"

"Current pop. Hard and fast and then slow, with a lot of rhythm."

He widened his grin, stood and held her chair. "Ladies first."

"That's what I'm hoping for."

Chapter 7

John held Mary tight to his side, and on occasion they swayed close to the railing. The slap-whoosh sound of the gentle waves hitting the side of the ship added a cadence during their walk. The ocean fragrance provided a romantic scent, while brown algae freed from the roots and clinging to driftwood, floated as ribbons on the calm surface. The pungent scent of sea spray as it sprinkled on their faces reminded him of how Mary had appeared cold and sweaty when she'd returned from the restroom. His heart jerked inside his chest at her suspicious behavior. Had she made contact with Peabody or Waterman, or a diamond buyer? She'd reentered the dining hall trailing a waiter, so her entrance had been through the kitchen. Why?

The puzzle became more complicated when she'd intentionally drank the wine. She'd sipped the dinner wine before, keeping in etiquette, but the dessert drink, a more powerful alcohol, she downed as if it were life-saving water and she was a thirsty castaway. At the bar last night she'd pretended to drink rum, but the beverage was alcohol free. Obviously, the woman wanted to keep her senses about her, and not be influenced by the debilitating effects of alcohol. What had changed between the time she left for the ladies room and now?

He'd had every intention of skipping out on dinner, but more than that he wanted to dance with her, to have an excuse to have their bodies aligned once again. His stomach tingled with need. Thankfully, she'd suggested leaving. He glanced at her, leaning her shoulder against the wall as he keyed the entrance to his room.

Her dreamy gaze pierced him. "Want to go into Kingston tomorrow with me? I need to get souvenirs for my friends."

"Sure." He rolled his fingers. "Come, my little pigeon."

"Sal Mineo or Charlie Chan?" She lifted an eyebrow.

"Sal Mineo."

She slipped past him. "I'm not dancing to jukebox music from the sixties."

Laughing, he locked the door. "I'll see what I can come up with."

Her purse clicked as it fell to the coffee table. She dropped her shoes where she stood.

John clicked on the music folder on his laptop; uninterrupted music would flood the room for at least two hours. Screen saver in place, he wouldn't worry about her discovering he'd bugged her room.

The snap of a clasp shutting together brought him around. Her lips were kissable shiny.

"Oh, I love this song, *Tattoo* by Jordan Sparks." She placed her hands between his shirt and coat and whipped the jacket off. Holding it like a matador, she flung the material over her shoulder to land beside her sparkling bag.

His hands automatically went to her waist, bringing her close. The hip to hip dance would begin. Her magic fingers undid the knot on his tie, and inch by inch she removed the silk from around his neck. It quickly followed the same path as the jacket. She'd flipped two buttons free from his shirt before he placed his palm on top of her hand.

"What's wrong?"

She flattened her fingers on his chest and swayed in time with the music. "Just making you comfortable. Do you like to dance?"

Stomach dropping, he inhaled, taking in her womanly scent which merged with the bouquet of her perfume. "Yes, my mother's a professional."

"Where?" She played with the edge of his shorn hair.

He turned her, so she wouldn't bump into the edge of the bed. "Hawaii."

"Your heritage is?"

"Fourth generation American." He didn't intend for the tone to be sharp, but sometimes discussing his heritage made him sensitive. Not that she'd shown any prejudices, but his name didn't appear in her journal either.

With a soft-callused finger, she stroked his right cheekbone. "Japanese?"

"Yes." They were in perfect sync. Her movement was sensuous, flowing with the rhythm of the song and igniting a fire inside him. Guilty of grand theft or not, he desired her and would have her.

She kissed the side of his face. "Which is why you're so beautiful."

"Thank you." He caressed her cheek with his. "What's wrong?"

"Did you know Rihana's song, *Take a Bow*," she nodded to the laptop, "playing now. It's about saying goodbye to a relationship? The couple gets along, but events go wrong and the romance doesn't work out."

To shake her secret free might loosen the connection between them and that would have been physically impossible. "Mary, tell me what happened when you went to the restroom."

She exhaled and shifted so their mouths were mere inches apart. "Will you kiss me?"

"Then will you answer my question?"

She blinked and shrugged. That her crimson dress was precariously close to exhibiting the rosy area of her nipples made his heart race in time with the music's beat.

"I'll take the chance." Intending to give her a light kiss, he gripped her face. He needed to touch the heart-shaped upper lip he'd been fantasizing about for two days, without hurting the injured one.

"I want one like you gave the cougar outside my room earlier today." Her arm around his neck tugged.

Mary was adorable--Debbie's age equaled hers. "What happened when you went to the can?"

"Saw a ghost." She outlined the shape of his mouth with her tongue, moving him to act on his desires.

He hesitated. What was her game? He took a step back.

"If you're not going to be serious." Heart thumping, pounding on his ribcage, John knew what he had to do. He released her, picked up her purse and shoes. "Good night, Mary."

True fear tightened her face. Pain glazed her eyes. "No. Please, I don't want to be alone tonight."

"Why?"

Arms folded at her waist, chin lowered, she whispered, "I'm afraid."

He flung her items and tucked her close. She had every reason to be scared. Two men who'd robbed her jewelry store were still at large and at this time, she wasn't clear from suspicion.

Swaying in time to the music, he tried to relax her. "What about now?"

Her cheek dropped against his shoulder. "I like Daughtry. He has a nice, raspy voice. We share the same taste in music."

"Do you believe in love? Quick, sharp, gut-wrenching love?" He kissed the soft skin of her shoulder.

"I want to believe. Mostly I've been disappointed. I hope..."

He lifted her arms to rest on his shoulders again, seeking that connection. "Yes, what do you hope?"

"I hope to find love before it's too late." She shook her head. "Most of the guys I've been attracted to don't stay. My last boyfriend was a scumbag." Her breath caught in her throat, making it sound like a sob. "I thought I saw a guy who looked like him in the hallway. Terrified me."

Her words floated in the air with spurts and sputters. Fear, true fright came from each word.

"If it was him, would he hurt you?" The slow removal of hairpins allowed the strands to flow down her back.

"He stabbed me here." Mary tapped John's heart. "A little theatrical. Sorry. Physically? Yes, I can imagine him getting angry and assaulting me." She shivered.

Rubbing her arms, he put his cheek against hers. "I'll protect you."

She kissed him, transforming that fear energy into passion. Her cupid lips hit the target, as if the love angel had shot his arrow. John Kajiyama confirmed he was in love with Mary Keefe.

He held her face in his hands. "You don't have to pretend an interest in me. I'll protect you." His words came out hard, but he didn't move away. "Maybe I should go look for the guy now."

* * * *

Mary whipped his hands away, but aligned her gaze with his. "No, I was wrong. That man couldn't be my ex. He's running from the law. I'm not faking romance with you in order to have safety. From the time I flattened you to the sofa, I've felt a spark. When you held me in the pool, embers flickered. I was hoping tonight I could see if a fire would ignite."

She was shocked the words had left her mouth. What had she been thinking, disclosing her past and then freely sharing her desire to be with him? She shouldn't consider a relationship with him. Love wasn't in the future for her. But a fling, one night to make the magic happen. Should she?

One night to feel the joy of being with this stunning man who looked at her as if she were the only female on a ship which appeared to have two women for every man.

One night to experience the enchantment of love.

"*Can't Fight This Feeling*," she whispered.

"Classic song for a classy woman," he replied and shifted, moving them into a dance again.

Face tucked near his neck, she breathed in his cinnamon spicy scent. He stroked her back, seeking and finding every crevice, exciting her and reigniting that spark.

"John," she drew his name out on a sigh.

His grip tightened as he pulled her closer, letting her feel what the spark activated. "Yes."

Hands low on his shoulders, she gazed into his eyes. "Could you kiss me now?"

His legs froze.

Any guy could get a boner after a fine meal, even better wine, and a ship filled with single hot women, so one of two things would occur: he'd pick up her shoes and purse and escort her into her room because he wasn't that into her, or he'd kiss her with passion.

A flick of her tongue wet her lips, but the action didn't relax her. She wished her heart wouldn't beat quite so hard. His glance went to her collar bone and then focused on her mouth again. *Please kiss me!*

His lips connected with hers. Slow and detailed, making her bottom lip plump with the attention and then he found the groove in her upper lip with his tongue and nothing, absolutely nothing would ever compare to his kiss. He quickly progressed from slow and searching to hard, fast, and breathtaking. His teeth clicked against hers and tongue parried with hers, and then he withdrew and sucked her mouth, pulling the tips of her lips she'd caught him staring at on several occasions. Arms wrapped around his neck, she tugged him so close their clothes were the only barrier to total satisfaction. She'd expected a flaming of embers. Instead, she'd gotten a raging inferno. A fire she didn't want to extinguish. Ever.

As she wove her fingers through his brown hair, the slide of zipper teeth separating the cloth of her dress sounded loud in the fraction of a second between songs. She sighed, knowing her fate was here, tonight with this man.

Chapter 8

Mary tugged John's white shirt, snapping the tails from his belted pants. Her dress had loosened when he'd unfastened the hidden zipper. A flap had fallen, doubling over and exposing one of her breasts. His soft insistent lips migrated from her neck to the crest of her nipple and in conjunction to her rioting hormones, her panties quickly grew moist.

He slid a hand between the dress sleeve and her skin, scooting the material farther down to rest at her waist.

Waves bashed against the outside of the ship, *slam, whoosh, slam, whoosh*, creating an equal rhythm in her lower body, pushing, pulling, imitating the wind pounding against the porthole. The threat of an impending storm didn't matter; the only thing that did mean something to her was connecting with this lovely man who made her feel wanted and desirable. Her clit quivered in anticipation. No sex for the past two months had deprived her, made her yearn for intimacy. She had his buttons undone and the sleeves shoved down to his elbows. "Yes, hard and fast."

He sucked air.

The dress rested at her waist. Had the garment caught on her hips? They were at a standstill, tethered in their own clothing. Together they gripped the silky material until it fell to her ankles. He unfastened the cuffs on his shirt and removed it and the tee underneath. She got busy. A snap and zip later, his trousers fell from his hips. A quick visual proved his size to be exceptional, rock hard and pulsating with life. Slipping her fingers under the band of his tight fitting boxers, she shoved them down his muscular thighs. His hands caressed her arms as she knelt, drawing her closer to his fully erect penis.

Her skin touched his, and the inferno boiled. His mouth latched onto hers. Thighs connected, they moved in sync until the backs of her knees bumped into the bed. A quick jerk to the covers exposed pristine white sheets. In her head, she lowered herself gracefully to the mattress and then posed in a sexy manner. Unfortunately the subliminal vision didn't play out. Having lost her balance, she plopped backward, bouncing slightly. Caught off guard, or because his foot stuck on any of the various pieces of slick clothing littering the floor, he fell on top of her.

Mirth gurgled in her throat. "Reminds me of when we met."

His cock vibrated between her thighs as he joined in the laughter. The solid power of him reminded her of his strength and how delicious his kisses were. She lost the amusement. Desire pulsated through her.

"Oh, please, now."

"Protection?" He pulled away.

"No."

"Not needed?" He nuzzled her breast, nibbling on her nipple and inched the rod about to give her so much pleasure closer. She opened her thighs, begging him to come into her.

"I don't have a condom, do you?"

He pressed his forehead against hers. "No."

"Are you willing to take a chance?" she whispered.

"I'm clean, are you?"

"Yes." His heaving breaths punctuated his words and blew pieces of hair away from her face. Should she tell him there would be a slight chance of pregnancy, or was that a given anytime people didn't have safe sex? Would he end their affair?

He sighed and smoothed her hair. The tip of his penis rubbed against her folds, making her wet and slick. "Please," she whispered and thrust her hips, hoping her bull's eye would meet his spear.

Swift and steady he pierced her, and moaned as she caught the rhythm. She held the screams of satisfaction inside, but released short bursts of air as the tension built.

His lips touched her face, neck, shoulder, and then clavicle. Each press equaled a thrust. The man kept his word. Hard and fast. By keeping the slap of their hips in time, she anticipated coming first, as promised.

Moans escaped. She bit her lip, trying to keep them contained.

"Let it go. Be yourself, love," he whispered, and then sucked on her earlobe, circling his tongue around the diamond stud. He slowed the rhythm, grinding and pressing as he drove himself inside her.

She shifted on the mattress, lifted and lowered herself.

"Whoa." His lips connected with hers, reigniting the fire, bringing her closer to climax.

Wait! The pleasure was too intense. She wanted their bond to last longer. "Yes, oh yes."

"Oh, yeah, love, what do you want?"

"You, only you." She gave in and rode the wave of the orgasm.

He drove deeper.

She lifted her hips, pressing against him and buried his manhood in her warmth.

He stopped, then slid to her hot spot again and ground harder, more slowly, every stroke sending jolts of sensation in a rush to her nerve endings. She wanted to shout as ecstasy overcame her, but didn't have the breath.

He stiffened, spending his seed. As the heat receded from the edge of her skin, she exhaled. Tiny currents continued to flicker inside her, sucking her deeper into the ecstasy rush.

Chapter 9

Feathery strokes tickling her cheek bothered her, but she could sleep through the pats. She'd slept through more than a little annoyance in the past. Spidy would just have to move on.

"Didn't you want to go into Kingston to shop for your friends?" a man said in a husky morning voice, titillating her ear drum.

Not a spider, but John. Mary rolled to the edge of the bed and peeled open her crust-laden eyelids. He stood in front of her dressed in khaki shorts, a white polo and a huge grin. Other than the funky looking Earth shoes, he was adorable. "Good morning. What time is it?"

"Nine. Ready to go?" He nudged her arm. "I have a little video camera. I'll tape our trip to port, so you can show your friends back in Keefe."

The mattress gave way as she flipped to her back and yawned. He had to be a Type A personality. Rules, regulations, and task driven. Time-consciousness was very important to her guy. Her stomach muscles tightened. He wasn't hers to have and to hold. She couldn't make any claim on him.

"Need help in the shower?"

She didn't want to leave the comfortable nest. If she moved, she'd have to think of today.

The day she had to run.

Her heart clutched at the thought. Not only would her life dramatically change, but the thought of leaving John when they were just beginning to know each other struck a painful blow to her core.

Her mouth tasted nasty, probably remnants of the wine she'd drunk. Her whole plan had come undone. Thank goodness her friends were observant enough to have created an escape clause. She shifted her legs to touch the floor with her feet, popped upright and jumped off the mattress. John, standing nearby, took a step backward. He'd probably never seen someone who went directly from asleep to awake in a moment's time. He stared at her as if trying to determine how she operated. No hope for him in this short amount of time. He'd just have to wonder.

Barenaked, she glanced around, seeking her clothes. They were neatly piled at the end of the coffee table. Okay, he was a little OC too...still adorable. "I'll shower. I'll be good to go in about thirty minutes."

The muscles in his throat moved up and down. "Good. I'll check my, ah, emails while you're..."

The man had to have seen a woman in naked form before, so why he acted like a teenager at a peep show confused her. "I'll return here once I'm ready."

His clever tongue wet his lips as he nodded. If only she had time for him to utilize that appendage in more diverse ways.

Gathering her stuff, she casually strolled into her room, shutting the door behind her. What to do first? Start the shower. A quick flip of the knob, and it sprayed. As the water splattered against the tiled walls, creating a sharp noise, she opened the closet. Jerking the backpack purse from the shelf, she stuffed a thin pair of jeans, a tee and underpants inside. She removed the key card from the purse and shoved the tiny jeweled handbag into an inside pocket. Where was her large handbag?

At the end of the couch. She rifled through, finding her wallet, cellphone, passport, and eyeglasses. All of the items fit in the little outside front-zippered pouch of the backpack. Face cream. Travel size toothbrush, paste and balm were buried down in the bottom of the bag, leaving a small amount of room. For her stylish expensive heels? Could she fit them in the tiny spot? Overstuffed, the sack might draw attention. Of course she'd need to buy a souvenir before she figured out how to escape, so she had to save space. She held a slim heel, outlined the red sole and touched the velvety soft surface. Damn. This was probably the first of many sacrifices she'd have to make because of her loser ex-boyfriend.

The shoe dropped, and Mary entered the shower. The razor was sharp and cut all of the wild hairs, making her free of bothersome fur for two days. She'd calculated at least forty-eight hours until she'd reach Vermont, depending on her source of transportation.

As she scrubbed her head, she created a plan. If time allotted and she could get through on her cellphone, she'd telephone Jenn to advise her to call her friend, Sasha Framee. Having an alternate arrangement for contact made her feel a little better. Maybe Jenn could tell Phoenix so she could notify her brother, Dane Bushard. Mary would have to dump the phone. The GPS could be tracked. Too much to think about. Her brain hurt.

She shut off the water and stepped out of the shower. John. What could she possibly do to let him know of her exit? A sob caught in her throat. Nothing. She couldn't tell anyone. They were on a cruise designed to help couples connect, so he'd find a new partner to ride the waves. Her focus had to remain on escaping. Conrad wouldn't stop. He'd track her until he took what he wanted. "Look where your mandate got me, Grandfather," she muttered into the mirror.

Mary quickly dried her hair and applied a sunscreen to her face. She'd picked up a nice tan the past two days, so other than some eye shadow, liner and mascara she was ready. Dressed in white slacks, a jewel blue sleeveless blouse, she added a long white overcoat. She could carry the jacket if it was hot, but traveling to Vermont, there would certainly be a change in weather so shorts were out. Money! Unable to open her backpack in front of John, she'd stuff money in her pockets for a souvenir and a taxi if needed. She had to make the trip look real. Removing her wallet from the slot, she took out a twenty, fifty and one hundred, which should be enough to cover all the costs.

Shoes? She sorted through her sandals. Black leather open toed, too tall for running. The blue pair were clacker heels, and she'd be heard a block away. Athletic shoes became her top pick. She tied the last knot on the laces, when a knock sounded on the connecting door. A quick fluff of her hair, and she wound her arms through the straps of the backpack. A sob stuck in her throat. She swallowed, forcing the angst back. In a few minutes she could lose everything: the store, her home, John and maybe even her life.

Courage, girl. The mantra played through her mind. Two steps and she pulled the door open. "Sorry, I know I took longer than I said."

John held the camera, which was only six inches long, in front of her. The extra hair-drying time was worth it as his glance traveled from her sneakered feet to her face. His gaze stopped at her lips for several seconds and then their stares connected. She reached out, intending to take his hand. Instead, he grabbed her arm and gently tugged her forward.

"You can take all the time you want, babe." He kissed her, the passionate *tongue down the throat* kind of lip lock she'd begged him for last night. In the light of day his mouth was more dangerous than during the romantic dance.

Several seconds later she broke the kiss and then caressed his cheek. "Thank you. I had a great time last night." She lowered her glance. "You're an exceptional lover."

No response from him, only light breathing. She braved a glance at his face.

He grimaced. What had she said wrong?

She stepped away and drew her sunglasses from her jacket pocket. "What do you think I should get my friends, shell jewelry, or scarves, or sarongs?"

"I can carry your purchases. You don't have to bring the backpack," he offered.

"I don't mind."

"It's going to be hot." John eased his fingers under one of the straps.

"I'd rather you keep your hands free, so..." She winked.

He heaved a sigh. "Let's stay here today. We can buy trinkets at the next stop."

She took his hand from under the canvas strap and rubbed her finger against his palm. "I need to go."

* * * *

Mary's glance fell after she made the odd remark. *Great time, like the sex was fun, but we're done* sort of comment. He took her hand and led her out the door, down the hallway and onto the elevator. "Tell me a little about your friends."

From her wide smile, her buddies meant a lot to her. "Phoenix, I've known since we were children. She looks a little like me with longer light brown hair and blue eyes instead of green, but otherwise we could be twins. She's an English teacher, and she's the best. Jenn works in an attorney's office and hopes to be a litigator someday." She laughed low in her throat, making him want to skip the shopping trip and give her another great time.

"She's trying to stop smoking, which means all of us are recipients of her sarcastic remarks. Kim is a physician, general practice. She has the sweetest, most beautiful little girls in the world. Oh, I need to pick up something for them. They'd probably like the shells. The ones you hold to your ear to hear the ocean." She squeezed his hand. "Remind me, 'cause I'll get lost in the scarves and jewelry."

"Okay." Why did he get the feeling she meant truly lost? He smiled and used his key card to exit the ship, waiting as she dug hers out of her pocket.

Mary continued to talk about her friends and how they'd formed a closer bond over the years. The information wasn't new to John, but needing to keep Mary talking in hopes she'd lower her shield, he asked questions. She'd erected a guard the moment he'd walked into her cabin and it had grown stronger as they'd presented their passport cards and exited the ship. Something filtered through her bright mind, and he was bound to find out what.

Sunrays made her hair brilliant with blond highlights. Her jacket would be coming off in the next hour. The temperature was at least ninety. The cobblestone main street was lined with vendors hawking wares of jewelry made from shells, bright floral patterned clothing, statues created from wood or other natural materials, and animals ranging from parrots to snails. Behind the stalls were buildings in a variety of jewel tone colors, bright yellow, orange, emerald green, sky blue. The city's promotional board had prepared for and presented exactly what a tourist was searching for in a visit to a tropical island.

Mary had found shells and exchanged funds. He took the bag from her outstretched hand when she came across some silky fabric large enough to be a dress. He truly didn't know the purpose for the garment, as one of the women wore a duplicate as a hair covering and another diagonally across her upper body. Must be a multi-purpose item.

As Mary began a bartering process, he took a few steps to evaluate a wallet. She was quite determined to get a better deal if she purchased three. Five minutes later, the seller lost her lyrical Jamaican accent and threw out the final price. Pleased, Mary shoved three of the articles and the sack John carried into her now overstuffed bag and replaced it on her shoulders. The vendor gave her change and Mary pressed the greenbacks into her pants pocket.

She slipped her arm through his. "I love getting a good deal."

A light touch of her lips on his was just enough that he felt the imprint of her beautifully curved upper lip. The Cupid's bow had fascinated him from the moment he'd seen photographs of the robbery. Now that he'd tasted her mouth and outlined the shape of her lips, committing them to memory, he couldn't get enough. He would never get enough of her.

"Oh look. Lovely. Are they real?" She skipped forward and picked up an orchid. The scent of the flower surrounded them. "So pretty."

"Not as pretty as you," he replied.

"Buy. Buy flowers for your wife," the short dark merchant insisted, as he shoved a bouquet into John's hands.

John glanced at her. Her eyes held a glint, as if she hoped he'd purchase them. Something else hovered beneath the surface. Fear? Illogical. What could she dread? A poisonous spider crawling out?

"Sure, I'll take a bunch." He'd just bought himself something to carry around the rest of the day, and her happiness.

Mary kissed his cheek. "You're sweet."

"As are you," he replied as the blossom monger wrapped up a fresh selection of orchids. John put the already wrapped bunch on the hawker's table and glanced at her, wanting to see her smile again.

Mary looked over his shoulder, and her eyes darkened. "I see some shell bracelets. I'll be on the other side."

A quick glance at the booth across the street proved it wasn't overly crowded. Only a few shoppers were meandering, so he nodded.

She slipped through a hub of people--their shipmates--and disappeared into an oncoming mass of new buyers.

"Thirty dollars," the thief demanded as he handed over the bouquet.

"Aren't orchids native to the area?" John handed over the cash.

The vendor winked and went to his next victim. Pocketing the money, he started his little scam set-up all over again.

John's phone rang. He waited for a break in the people traffic to cross and join Mary before answering.

"John, I reviewed the footage you asked me to look at last night and found our guy," Debbie said on the other end. "Peabody was one of the calypso musicians performing every night at the pool down from your room." Her heavy breathing passed through the phone.

"I looked at the band members, didn't see him." A cramping in his stomach started, an unease about what could occur ripped through his mind. Mary had told him last night she'd seen the ghost of her ex. Instead of acting on his sleuthing instinct, he'd seduced her. Damn.

"He didn't look anything like his photo. He completely changed his appearance with dreadlocks, darkened his skin, maybe some minor plastic surgery." She took a breath and stopped. "Where are you?"

Hot! Hot! Hot! The song currently played on the steel barrels made his heart beat at a faster rate. Grilled meat mixed with the orchids made him nauseous. He couldn't see Mary. "On the main street, by the drums."

"I hear them." Debbie's harsh breaths pounded his ear. "Is Keefe with you?"

His heart rammed into his chest. Where was she? "She's at one of the booths. Why?"

"Conrad got off the ship. He's in the village with you. They could be meeting to hand off the diamonds."

"Fuck." John dropped the flowers and took off running.

"Bang Wang! Bang Wang," Mary screamed.

Chapter 10

Mary's only chance to escape presented itself while John was hidden behind a woven straw hat vendor. She'd taken several hurried steps, then an arm had wrapped around her neck, forced her against the side of the structure closest to the alley. Sharp edges of the brick had bitten into the back of her hand as her knuckles hit the surface. Axe cologne had filtered into her nostrils.

Conrad. His switch blade had snapped as it clicked into place.

"Bitch. Thought you'd escape," he'd said. Sharp, cold metal had pressed into her skin.

"I'll tell you," she'd begged, "what I did with them."

He'd loosened the pressure on the knife.

Then she'd screamed. *Please God, let John hear my cry for help.* He'd set the safety shout-out. John would save her.

"Fuck you." Conrad slid the blade into her skin. Blood gushed.

"Mary!" John yelled. The urgency in his voice made the attack surreal.

The pressure from the knife lessened. Conrad turned toward the shout. Mary took advantage, swiveled and kicked him in the balls. Slipping from his grasp, she stumbled a few steps.

"ACI. Throw down your weapons, Peabody!" John shouted from behind her.

A crushing blow, even more painful than the knife to her throat jammed her heart. John knew Conrad. Therefore, he had to have been investigating her. What was ACI? The law? Regardless, she'd meant nothing to him except as a suspect. All along, he'd wanted to find Conrad and the jewels.

Mary took off running down the alley, keeping in the shadows. She glanced behind her to witness Conrad fighting John. She tried to block out John shouting her name, but the mantra stayed with her. "Stop. Don't run, Mary."

Her heart beat painfully inside her chest. Her throat hurt, but she had to keep going. No turning back now. Bright light blinded her as she ran from the dark alley. She stumbled, nose first, into a banana tree. Grabbing hold of a limb for balance, a leaf came off. She held the cool soothing foliage to her burning neck, hoping to stop the trickle of blood. After a few blinks to adjust her sight, she searched for a taxi. Cars were everywhere, but none had a sign indicating cab.

She grabbed her phone from her pocket, blood smearing on her white jacket as she extracted the cell. Her shaking fingers slipped across the keys. Thank God Jenn had keyed the number in already.

"Yeah," a man said in a deep musical voice that rang true and clear.

"Sasha, its Mary, Phoenix's friend. I need a cab to get to your house. How do I hail one? None of the cars say taxi."

"Where are you?" His smoky voice held an island rhythm, immediately relaxing her a bit.

She glanced behind her to the alley, free of John and Conrad. She didn't know which one had won the confrontation. A quick glance both ways, and she moved to the other side of the massive tree taking up three-fourths of the sidewalk. The buildings were marked with numbers but no names. Holding the leaf to her throat, she kept to the shadows and walked farther away from the ocean, the vendors and John. "Kingston, next to the Blue Cafe."

"Stay there, I'm five minutes away. I'll be driving a yellow VW Bug."

"Hurry." She fled behind the building and slumped against the brick wall. Blood continued to flow down her neck, when she stuffed the phone into the side pocket of her backpack. The burning pain receded slightly as she shoved the cool plant against her throat.

Sirens sounded a street away. Would the cops--along with John, or if she were truly unlucky, Conrad--be looking for her? How could she hide wearing white stained with blood?

She dropped the leaf and removed the backpack. Shrugging the jacket off, she placed the purse onto her shoulders again. Pressing the edge of a sleeve to the wound, she used the hem of the coat to dab her shirt, trying to soak the crimson liquid. The blood smelled like sulfur, making her nauseous. The white material darkened to a brownish-red. Light headed, she hoped Sasha would arrive before she passed out.

Fingers tight against the cut, she held the now scarlet sleeve away from her body. If one of the workers from the restaurant came out, he or she would surely call the police. Her heart pounded at an unsteady, fast rate, either because of the blood loss or fear of being discovered. The sound of an engine purring brought her away from the wall. She glanced into the street. Yellowish-orange VW car with a dark-skinned driver. He flagged her forward, and then threw open the door.

Mary flung the coat toward the Dumpster and ran. Inside the car, she leaned forward to accommodate her backpack and slammed the door. Her bent position made the wound spurt. Blood gushed onto his carpet, making her dizzy and sick. Frozen with horror, she reacted by sticking her palm to the injury.

"I'm sorry. Do you have a cloth so I can stop the bleeding?" she said. Her voice was scratchy. Had her vocal cords been cut? She didn't know enough to self-diagnose. She only knew she was going to be violently ill.

"Damn." Focused on driving, he must not have noticed the geyser. He spun the car around and headed in the opposite direction. Driving at rapid speed, he maneuvered around slow moving and parked cars. The brakes squealed as he jolted to a stop at a light. "Lean back."

She closed her eyes and awkwardly pressed against the seat. A small car and a large backpack made for a tight space. The snap of a compartment opening and papers shifting came to her. Air. She must have air, and wrapped her fingers around the window roller.

"Here." A cloth squashed into her palm. She sucked in a breath and smashed the fabric against the cut.

"Thanks. Sorry about the carpet." Unable to control the light-headed weakness, she swallowed the vomit in her throat. "Sasha...I'm going to pass out now."

* * * *

John snapped the plastic band handcuffs on Peabody's wrists, then flipped the safety latch on the pistol, and slid it into the ankle holster. "Where's your partner in crime?"

"She left."

Peabody meant Mary, but he lied. "Where is your real conspirator? Waterman. Tell me where the diamonds are."

"I don't know what you're talking about." He plopped onto the sidewalk and leaned his head between his knees.

"Is he nearby? Did he take Mary?"

Peabody shook his head. "No. I liked Mary. I didn't mean to cut her so deep. God, the blood. So much rushed out, like a damn faucet full open."

John couldn't catch his breath, a result of the physical activity or seeing Mary gushing blood. Either way, he needed to find her. She could be... No, not dead. He couldn't think like that. Critically wounded.

"She's dead, isn't she?" Peabody asked. Damn, why did he have to voice it? Vocalizing the possibility only made it seem real.

"John?" Debbie skidded to a stop in front of them. The crowds hadn't dissipated, but huge numbers of people didn't hover around them, either. It was as if the knifing and fight hadn't occurred. Women laughed. *Banana Boat* currently rang from the steel drums and peddlers hawked their goods. The urge to cut and run made John anxious. He needed to find Mary.

The Kingston police, dressed in khaki shorts and capped shirts, arrived on motorcycles.

"What's going on here?" A cop who could have been a suntan lotion model stared at Peabody trussed like a turkey with blood smeared on his hand and shirt. Mary's blood. "Hand over your weapons."

John bent and unsnapped his gun holster. "I'm John Kajiyama and this is Debbie Gilbert. We're with Atlantic Coast Investigations. I have privileges to carry a weapon. The paperwork is in my back pocket. This man, Conrad Peabody attacked a woman, slit her throat. He's also wanted for grand theft in South Carolina. The proper authorities will need to be informed." He extended his gun, butt first.

"He attacked the woman in Kingston?" The cop was clever. If taken on his turf, the local police would keep him.

"Yes, and robbed a jewelry store in South Carolina," John reiterated.

"Serg, there's blood over here. Looks fresh," a dark-skinned, thin officer said.

Serg lifted an eyebrow. "Injured?"

"Mary Keefe, the victim, escaped Peabody and darted down the alley." John wasn't going to declare she'd ran from him. His gut clenched at the thought she'd felt the need to run. "Could your men scan the area? Light brown hair and green eyes, five eight, about one hundred and twenty pounds. White suit. Backpack."

Serg evaluated John for several minutes, then removed the radio from his belt clip and gave the instructions over the device.

"Let's go to the station and talk details." Serg nodded to the skinny officer. "Get that cleaned up. We don't want our visitors disturbed from spending their holiday on the island."

* * * *

John displayed his credentials and provided the contact information, including the police detective he worked with in Keefe, South Carolina. At the police station, he filed a report and left Debbie to deal with clean-up. They located Mary's jacket a block away, blood soaked. No sign of *j.j. Keller*

Mary and not one person they interviewed had seen her running through the street or at the cafe. She had to have had a contact on the island. John would need to run a report to determine her last phone calls.

Back on the ship, he went through Conrad Peabody's room, and found nothing but a note to meet one of the kitchen staff at midnight.

Peabody's partner-in-crime comment rushed through his mind. He went to his room, packed up his equipment and carried it into Mary's cabin. Deciding to start by sorting clothes to see if he could find clues to her innocence, he opened the closet door.

Three loud raps shook the cabin door frame. He rushed through the narrow passageway and answered. A customer service agent held three large packages in his arms.

A skinny hand appeared from behind the cumbersome containers. "Here are your boxes, sir. I'm Jared Knox, I'm to wait for you and help you carry them off the ship."

"Thanks. It'll be awhile."

The pimple faced kid lowered the cartons to the floor. "Sir, I was asked to help you speed the process. We need to exit the port at oh-five-hundred."

"Fine. Did you bring packing tape and a marker?"

In less than twenty minutes, they had Mary's personal items packed and sealed. John signed documents allowing him to take her possessions. Jared carried the labeled boxes, to be delivered to the ACI office, off the ship and John loaded them into a taxi.

John's stomach roiled and his heart pounded as fast as the steel drums beating out a rapid tune. Had Mary been killed and they'd find her body buried in the tobacco fields or in the ocean?

Chapter 11

Water lapping against the side of the hull woke her. Mary opened her eyes. She wasn't in her stateroom on the cruise ship. She rolled to her side. Pain pierced her neck, arms and legs. Using her elbows she came upright, then pressed a hand to her throat and slowly shifted from the bunk to land on her feet. A window was to her left. She only had to turn her head an inch or so and she could see outside. Bruised skin pulled tight, then a squirt of liquid flowed from her wound. At least she was alive.

From the porthole, she gathered it was night. No stars and no running lights on the boat. Where was she?

She glanced around, finding the exit, and unsteadily walked toward the source of fresh brine-scented ocean air. As she passed a mirrored door, she stopped. Her neck had a bandage wrapped around and tied in a knot at the back. She had to look at the cut and peeled the edge of the bandage.

"Don't. We just got it to stop bleeding," Sasha said from behind her.

She jerked, bumping her hand against her jaw. "I just wanted to see how bad it is."

"Lots of blood loss, but the slice will heal fine." He wrapped his thin ebony fingers around her arm. His fine brown hair appeared wet, as if he'd taken a swim. "Come, sit down and I'll get you some juice. You'll need to rebuild your energy."

She took a seat on the bunk she'd just vacated. "Where are we?"

"Outside Miami, Florida. I've arranged fare for you on a train, Amtrak I think, to Vermont. You have a private passenger car with only one change over and that's in Chicago." His lyrical voice ebbed and flowed with a rhythm as sweet as the juice she was about to consume. He placed a small glass of orange liquid with lots of pulp in front of her. "Drink."

The red-orange thick liquid had a pungent odor, reminding her of seaweed. "Where's my bag? I have a change of clothes in it."

j.j. Keller

"It's at the end of the bunk." He retrieved a black satchel and plopped it on the table. "However, you're not going to wear jeans." His black eyes glimmered. Jenn was right; this man had all the attributes of a very sexy donor.

He must have transferred her stuff from the backpack to the bag. Skeptical, she took a drink. "I'm not?"

He shook his head, his product-slicked wet hair not moving. Drops of water slid from the strands, landing on his plain green tee shirt. A little lower and the liquid would have landed on his protruding nipples. The guy worked out.

"No. In order for you to remain hidden, you're going to wear…" His muscles bunched under his khaki shorts as he pivoted and reached inside the closet. "…this."

She lowered the somewhat tasty beverage to the nearby table, and raised an eyebrow. "Because it goes so well with the bandage?"

He laughed, a deep throat-vibrating chuckle. "No one will bother you if you're dressed like a nun, and hopefully you won't have to show ID, just your ticket."

"Fine. I don't care. I'm tired." She laid her head on top of the pleather bag and looked at him.

He winked, a slow, steamy eye catching move. Just as Jenn had predicted, the man was sex personified. A black robe and Egyptian-style hat landed on the chair. "Thirty minutes. You'll need to get changed, and remove those earrings."

"Yeah, I'll be ready."

He strode up the stairs and outside, leaving the door open. As if weights were tied to her ankles, she dropped her hand to the tabletop and stood. A quick sort through the bag proved everything was present, even the cash she had stashed in the cellphone pocket. But where was her mobile?

She loaded the items back inside the satchel. Her clothes had hardened with blood, which scratched her skin. Carefully she eased the blouse and slacks from her body. Brownish red smears trailed from her right shoulder down to her waist. Dried crusts of blood flaked from her panties, falling to the floor as she walked. She went into the bathroom, grabbed a clean cloth, removed her underwear and quickly washed her skin. A quick scrub to her bra and panties, then she rolled them in a towel to get them as dry as possible. With the water squeezed out, she wrapped them in a hand towel and traded dry undergarments for the semi-wet ones.

Dressed in the black gown, she knotted her hair and whipped the handkerchief hat onto her head. The piece fit tight on her forehead, making her look dowdy, pale and unkempt.

"Ready?" Sasha whipped his gaze around her, inspecting.

"Where's my cellphone?"

The motor cut, the boat slowed, causing the waves to hit the hull harder, throwing her off balance.

He gripped her arm. "I had to deep six it about five miles outside Kingston. The phone has a GPS, and we didn't need to be tracked."

"Also, the pay-as-you-go?"

He nodded.

Her heart clutched. She'd planned to get rid of it once she'd contacted her friends. They wouldn't know what happened to her. Maybe the news had a spot about an attack on a passenger from the ship on Kingston. They would be worried. "So I'll be without communication for forty-eight hours? Will you call Jenn?"

"I did. Your friends are aware you're safe. Stay in your passenger car. We have enough food packed for three days. You won't need to go out except to change trains in Chicago."

"I understand. What about the neck?"

Sasha lifted an eyebrow, a glint crossing through his wide-eyed stare.

She lifted an index finger toward the slice on her throat.

"We did the best we could. Cleaned the four inches, slapped steri-strips and wrapped the gauze around. You might get an MD to look at it." He pulled the material higher on her neck. "Come on, we've docked. The cops will be searching for your backpack as an identifier for you. Let's hope they won't look twice at a nun."

* * * *

John paced, his already-small apartment shrinking with each step. He stopped in front of Mary's clothing pile, picked up a blousy thing and sniffed it. Her scent--perfume and her own personal smell--remained on the material. An image of her dancing and the sweet exhilaration as she'd climaxed under him. He tossed the garment on the stack and moved to the jewelry. Traveling crate in hand, he sat on his black leather sofa, placing the box on the glass coffee table. The latch came free. Obviously the case had been frequently used. Simple designs in silver and one set of gold earrings rested on black velvet inside.

He picked up a triangle-shaped necklace. Scrolls and leaves were embedded on the outer rim. A blue stone, the color of the water outside of his parent's beach house was set inside the trinket. He held it to his lips, trying to connect with her through her personal possessions.

Mary wasn't dead. He wouldn't believe it until he touched her cold hard body. Somehow she'd escaped and sought refuge. Peabody had been captured, but his partner remained at large. She had every reason to be afraid. But what if she'd had the diamonds all along?

John put the necklace back in the square. He clicked on the music folder. A song rang through the room as he gathered a pen and paper from inside the glass and chrome desk. He re-positioned on the sofa. One knee drawn upward to hold the pad, he closed his eyes and enjoyed the song. The very music they'd danced and made love to filtered through his mind. Momentarily taking his thoughts away from sorting and categorizing information, he relived the small fraction of time they'd shared. Their bodies had finally connected after two days of verbal foreplay.

Hot anger ripped through him. He would find Waterman before the deviant found Mary.

Her items had been logged at the police station and at his home office, but he'd dragged the luggage home. He had hoped to discover something, anything that would provide him a clue as to where she'd gone. He grabbed her notebook and reread the entries. Likert Scale of one through five was easy enough to understand. She sought a future boyfriend and her questions, while odd, did lead him to believe she was searching for a partner.

Pages fluttered as he slipped through looking for other leads. Text on the first three pages, then the data she'd started to accumulate. The bartender, his name had hearts above the I. DONOR…D rated a solid four, O had a four plus, N equaled five, A the number five with two stars nearby and R only had *question Jenn* beside it. The next entry was the First Mate, who rated all fives and three hearts. Then testosterone guy ranked three or less on all entries. Clearly the First Mate had all the points, if five was the highest, and from John's point of view the First Mate was the best of the three. John evaluated each sheet in the rest of the book, searching for embossed writing from where a page had been torn out. Nothing.

Where was his entry? Hadn't she considered him as a prospective candidate?

The vibrations from his phone brought him out of the disappointment lull. "Kaj--

"John, GPS took us to the sea," Debbie said. "No doubt her phone is at the bottom. Either she was taken by someone and they dumped the cell overboard, or Keefe herself ditched it so she couldn't be found."

John frowned. "How much blood did the docs estimate she'd lost?"

"All right. So she was taken."

"How much?" His voice had a chill. Debbie wouldn't argue with him, knowing he expected answers.

She gave a long drawn-out sigh. "Enough she couldn't walk around on her own. Before you ask, we're keeping in contact with all the nearby hospitals, the one on the island and various points on the mainland. If she shows up at a medical facility, then we'll know."

"Did the police get any information from Peabody?" John wasn't surprised the detectives let her be involved with the interrogation. She'd been with the FBI for a short period of time and she had a way of working a suspect.

"Nothing of consequence. He keeps mumbling about killing Mary. Poor sweet Mary." A soft snort came across the connection. "He did take a breath to ask me to post bail."

"He didn't volunteer where the diamonds had been hidden?" John set the journal and pad of paper on the end table.

"No such luck. He's close to disclosing his partner, though. I'm dying to tell him we already know, but I want to find out what his threshold is." She chuckled low in her throat.

"I'm glad you get your rocks off by mentally torturing detainees." John sorted through the jewelry, selected a thick S-link bracelet with tiny 'I's and 'O's engraved on each link. A beautiful example of her craft, she was extremely talented.

"Do you want me, once I'm all hot and bothered? We could finish what we started on the ship." She sounded serious.

He reached under his white t-shirt, scratched his stomach and then tugged the string on his lounge pants. "Debbie, you know when I kissed you I was trying to get Mary--"

"Just messing with you, Kajiyama." Although she added a joking lift at the end, her tone sounded wistful.

"Oh. Good night then, I'm going to search for clues." John, on bare feet, moved to his desk and sat in the upholstered chair. He removed the MP3 and drew up his databases. To find Mary, if she was hiding from Peabody or his partner, he had to track down her friends. The way she'd talked about them, they meant a lot to her. Mary's intimate group would lead him to her.

He had to drive to South Carolina.

Chapter 12

Mary snuck a peek at Mrs. Landware, who pulled Frank to the side near one of the rough plank walls of the shop. Outside the window, past the whispering couple, Mary could see enormous pine trees, Douglas fir if she remembered her Pine Trees 101 lesson correctly. The dark green flat leaves encircled the branches and mixed well with oak, maple and beautiful red cedar trees. The frost-edge lined panes added character to the winter scene. The state of Vermont in November was stunning. Artificial Christmas trees with blinking LED lights near the edge of the carpet runner decorated the store entrance. Snowfall was promised which would add background ambiance for the setting through the massive windows. Each time the door opened, chilled air brought fresh balsam-pine scent of live evergreens into the gardening store. The fragrance mingled with cinnamon sticks and mums, sweetly taking her back to her family childhood Christmases, when life was simple.

"Frank, I want to talk to you about the new girl." The tiny green velvet hat shifted on the petite woman's small, tightly-wound white curls. A cream blouse peeked from under her emerald wool coat. Black flaps of high boots brought the ensemble together, making Mrs. Landware resemble the Travelocity elf standing among the fake trees. Multicolored speckles flickered, casting a rainbow around her pale face.

"Yes, Mrs. Landware, I'll be happy to discuss our store. As for Mary, she has only been with us two weeks." Frank glanced at Mary and winked.

The Christmas train on a track installed near the crown molding let off a whistle as it passed overhead. Mary's heart relaxed a little. She loved this job and certainly couldn't find another in such close proximity to her current place of residence. The Garden and Floral Design Center was a mile from Phoenix's brother Dane's guest house, which enabled her to walk or ride Dane's 1950s bicycle. Cage, Vermont was Kinsdale painting perfect, and she planned to start a new life here. Even if she was cleared of the jewel heist, she'd stay. A fresh start.

The mothball-scented woman wagged her finger at Frank. He shifted to stand closer to the miniature pencil Christmas trees near the display window of the store, and to Mary's dismay, a little farther from eavesdropping range. His bald head shone in the dim lights as he bent as much as possible over his portly belly to reach for a fallen tin soldier from the cream and brown tiled floor.

"She's wonderful. I want her to create all of my floral arrangements in the future." Mrs. Landware nodded toward her and then tugged Frank's lapel, pulling him within inches of her lined face. "Can I have her for an entire weekend to decorate my house for the holidays? Relatives are coming in a couple of weeks and staying until Christmas."

"I'm sure we can make arrangements for her to create floral designs for your home." Frank untangled her fingers from his jacket. Straightening his bent spine, he shoved his hands into his pockets.

"This weekend, she can come to my house and see what we're dealing with." Mrs. Landware waved her hands. Tim, the carry-out boy, hoisted the large American red rose and baby's breath bouquet wrapped in cellophane and followed her.

The double doors shut, leaving a tinkling of bells in its wake and a fresh rush of North Woods scent.

Frank pivoted.

Mary quickly refocused on the partially arranged fresh flowers, turning the container to check all the sides for equality and balance. Fall shades, full and vibrant reds, oranges, and ochre, autumn colors were at their best. The scents, undeniably unique to the north, were refreshing to a southern gal.

"You heard?"

She glanced away from the pungent lilies. "I believe Marvin out in the cut balsam trees area could have heard."

"Do you want to do the special project?" Despite his age, Frank had some vibrancy in his movements, as proved by the sudden bounce of his heels. He could often be heard validating his love of life, and it showed in every word spoken or action taken.

"Of course. I'm not sure where she lives, but if I can get there by bicycle, I'll go." Floral arrangement complete, she placed the container in the refrigerator. "She's a sweet lady."

"You can use one of the Center's vans." He glanced around the interior of the store and then out the large bay window. "You have a driver's license, right?"

"Yes." A swipe to clear away the debris on the surface of the dark gray granite work counter, and she took the orange cleaner and a fresh rag in hand. She sincerely hoped he believed her and did not insist on seeing her license. Dane had helped her to obtain the job. He hadn't divulged what was said, but Frank hadn't argued when she'd asked for her pay to be in cash. Curious maybe, but he'd held the questions inside. Mary had promptly created a Frank-the-prior-gangster scenario in her head to explain why he didn't query the oddness of her request of payment.

"Great, once Landware gets the word out, we'll have more opportunities." Behind his glasses, his eyes shimmered with dollar signs. "Lots of holiday bonuses for us."

Frank strutted to the window and slapped his hand on the wood base. "Betty hasn't started working on this. Will you finish the display while you're here today?"

"Yep. Got a cute idea. Should I pass it by Betty first?" Betty, the other floral designer, didn't like 'having that girl around'. Mary had overheard that conversation. *"The new girl doesn't know flowers."* Which was true, but Mary knew design. Whether the materials came from gold, silver or a glass case holding blooms, she could work them into an attractive object, because she needed beauty in her life.

"No. When she comes in this afternoon, send her to me." Frank took a step toward his office and stopped. The scarred antique oak door gleaming from a recent waxing reflected his grin.

"Devon, good day. Here for your weekly floral arrangements?" Frank tapped him on the back.

Mary had encountered Dr. Devon Buckley three previous times. He was an attractive man, six-foot, pure silver hair, a couple of wrinkles around his eyes, and straight white teeth. The Richard Gere look-a-like had jumped from the movie screen and stood in front of her cold flower fridge, making her heart thump in joy at viewing such splendor.

Dr. Buckley shook Frank's hand. "Yes. I must admit I like the new bouquets you've got on hand." Despite his deep voice, he was soft spoken. Almost like he was comfortable with himself, his life, and no one could disrupt his zen. "I've been here a few times recently."

"I think it's the new girl," Frank stage-whispered.

Dr. Buckley glanced at her and smiled, just the corners of his mouth going upward. They both knew she was way beyond "girl" status, but since Frank Cartwright was at least sixty-five, he could get away with calling her a girl.

The knot on her scarf hiding the large bandage covering her wound slipped as she turned to get a vase. Once the container was on the counter, she moved the cloth up, then extracted a dozen yellow roses from the tub in the bottom of the fridge.

"I'll let you get to your business, Frank. It was nice seeing you." Dr. Buckley edged close to the work station. "You know me already, Mary?"

Heat rushed to her face. Had she unconsciously disclosed her admiration for his beauty? "You're a regular, Dr. Buckley."

"I thought we agreed you'd call me Devon." He extracted a greeting card from the acrylic stand on the counter with his lean, nimble fingers and wrote on it like he always did. Devon would ask her to place it in the fresh roses just as he had the last three times.

"Sorry. Devon, will this arrangement work for you?"

He didn't look at her or the flowers, but nodded and continued writing on his card. All right, anything would be good, which meant the man wasn't picky or he trusted Frank's employees would give him nothing but the best. Maybe she could toss a bunch of thistles in a vase and he'd say, "I like it." Who did he give the flowers to? No wedding ring in place…did he have a wife? A man that handsome had to have a woman by his side.

"Mary, I couldn't help but overhear Mrs. Landware's request. I'd also be interested in having you decorate my house. My son is a freshman at Stanford and has been gone for several months. I'd like this Christmas to be special, a welcome home. Do you think we could make arrangements?" He stared with his dark brown eyes as if searching for something hidden.

"Sure. I'd like that. What's your son's name?" She finished wrapping the flowers and tucked the arrangement and bundle in a bag to keep them safe from the sharp, cold wind. Snow was predicted. She couldn't wait. Growing up in the south provided her limited experience with the fluffy white stuff.

He extended the card. "Eric. He's interested in finance." Her hand tightened on the bundle. "Next week I'll bring some dates that would work for me."

Tucking the white parchment inside the bouquet, she held out the sack. "Fine. I'll look forward to making your house special for your family."

Devon went through the exit and Mary started working on the window display. Joy at the compliment Frank had given her, considering she had zero experience at floral design, would last for several days. In the past three weeks of living in Cage, she'd learned the people of the community were honest and old-fashioned. She loved their quirky witticisms and the little tidbits of wisdom they'd shoot her way.

Sorting through the storage closet, she found a strand of lights shaped like candles. Several boxes later she found replacement corms, and after testing each one and changing the bulbs, the wired decoration worked perfectly.

As agreed earlier, Tim, the high school kid who worked part-time, tacked pine boughs to the window frame. Dane had promised to deliver an old tricycle and antique grizzly bear from his attic, which would be the centerpiece of the display. She'd passed the idea by Betty when she'd called in sick.

Tim left to help a customer. Mary strung lights and crimson berries through the greenery. The fresh pine scented the area with crisp hope. She'd give the Cage residents a Dickensian Christmas, complete with white poinsettias to act as snow. She went outside and glanced at the window. Tonight she'd pull some vines from the woods to add a little rustic brown.

"Hey Mary, Mr. Bushard dropped these boxes off. He said he was in a hurry, something about a dinner with blah blah blah. Where do you want them?" Tim tugged two large boxes in front of the entrance.

"Could you put them near the window inside, please?"

Tim nodded.

"Thanks, buddy." Chilled, she rubbed her arms and followed him.

Tim unpacked the tricycle, bear and a child's rocking chair. Thrilled at the decorating possibilities, she hoped the bay window ledge might have just enough room for all three.

Mary situated the items on the pristine sheet masquerading as snow, then the white poinsettias and added holly sprigs here and there to fill the gaps.

Boxes folded, Tim flipped the *Closed* sign on the windowed door. "Hey, Mary, need a ride home?"

Tim drove a small truck, which seemed to sit low to the ground. At night, blinking lights appeared underneath. He was always willing to hoist her bike into the back and give her a lift.

"That would be fantastic, I'm wiped out. Just let me close out the cash register." A glance at the sales total, and she compared it to the money banked. They equaled. She zipped the bag, unplugged the lights and walked toward the office.

"I'll put your bike in the truck while you hand over the goods to Frank." Tim gave a two-fingered wave and rushed out the back door.

Frank, naturally a chatty person, was on the telephone as she placed the bank bag on the desk. She waved good-bye to him, silently thanking the caller on the phone, and rushed to the coat rack.

Grabbing her borrowed anorak, Mary slid into the garment and pushed the sleeves up. Dane had found the coat in the attic and mentioned the bear and the child's bike. He'd agreed to let her borrow them to decorate the guest house. Now they were going in the center's window.

Double-checking the store, she unplugged an electric candle and rushed outside to the truck. Tim, settled behind the massive steering wheel, bobbed his head to the loud country music, pounding against the dash. A nod and he unlatched her door. The cold metal squeaked, echoing off the trees as it squealed open. The muted blue metal cracked off, exposing the rusted structure underneath.

She climbed onto the split black leather seat and placed the belt across her waist. "Thanks again for the ride," she shouted.

The decibels went down to human level. "No problem. Like I said before, your house is on my way."

A few minutes later he pulled into the lane leading to her temporary home. Tim threw the gear into park and jumped from the cab. As he removed the bike from the back end, she got out of the cab and joined him. "Here you go, Mary. Good night."

"Good night, Tim. Thanks." The bike, easy to guide but suddenly heavy, stuck in the land ruts. She sluggishly pushed it forward and leaned the two-wheeler to rest against the rough logs of the guest house. As she unlocked the door, she envisioned a long bubble bath, followed by a soothing foot rub and a cup of soup with hopes to warm up before she gathered vines. Maybe she'd cut back the creepers from the grape arbor, which was closer than the woods. Anxious to get inside the building, she tried to ignore the footsteps pounding on the brick path behind her.

"Mary!" Dane shouted.

Exhale, she told herself, and half-pivoted, keeping beside the door. Her hand, ready to pull the lever, didn't waver. He swiped his longish brown hair from in front of his periwinkle blue eyes and smiled. "Did you get the boxes of toys?"

"Yes, thank you. What's up?" She flung the door open and placed her keys in the dish on the small foyer table. A few minutes and a couple of steps, and she'd be lounging in that sweet claw-foot tub. In the meantime, she unbuttoned her coat.

"I--Alex and I--were hoping you'd come to dinner. We have a setting for eight and the female just canceled. I need an eighth, and a woman." He bit his lip as if afraid she'd say no.

She couldn't respond with a negative. Dane and his partner, Alex, had invited her to live in their guest house rent free and for as long as she needed. "Sure. When?"

"One hour. Do you have a dress? Something more formal?" He raked his glance down her tee shirt and jeans. She didn't have a great selection of clothing. Being on the run limited what items could be transported. An instant image of her cayenne red dress left in her cabin on the ship flew into her mind. Thoughts of John followed. She had to get him out of her head. They'd had a one night stand, period.

"Nope." Her throat closed, she coughed to clear it. "I'm sorry. When I get paid I'll buy a few bits and pieces."

He grinned. "No worries, Phoenix always leaves clothes here. She's taller than you, but in a dress it probably won't matter. I'll select something and bring it over."

"Great. I'll be in the tub, so just leave it on the bed."

Dane's dry hands rubbing together, resembled the crunch of leaves. Bouncing from foot to foot in front of the door, he turned to leave. "I'll be back in a few minutes. You've one hour."

"Good. I'll be ready. Oh, and Dane, I'll need heels."

He nodded and hurried down the sidewalk.

Mary shut the door, toed her shoes off and strode into the bathroom. With the black rubber disc inserted into the hole, she started the water, adding a dollop of citrus scented bath beads. Vermont was bone-chilling cold maybe the summers would be hot. She'd adjust, because there wasn't any going back to her home.

Her heart clutched. Her parents existed in her heart and mind and not the physical structure she'd called home. Now, she was alone without mementos to help remember the good times. Besides, she loved the people of Cage.

Clothes off, Mary glanced in the gold ornate mirror above the sink to remove the kerchief. Next, she peeled off the bandage. The knife cut was ugly. Jagged edges with a bump in the middle, open and leaking. The two ends of the four inch cut had sealed over, but the center refused to heal.

Mary crawled into the tub and dipped her head under the water, then lifted to rest the back of her neck along the edge. Eyes closed, she relaxed, feeling the muscles slowly unwind in each part of her body.

The creak of a door opening brought her back from serenity. Crap, out of relax time. She smeared soap on top of the loofah and scrubbed, then released the drain and washed her hair under a fresh stream of water. Wrapped in a towel, she climbed from the tub and combed her hair, tossing the wet strands over her shoulder. A quick glance in the mirror showed blood ran from the cut like chicken broth in a sieve. She grabbed a tissue from the box decorating the toilet tank and dabbed at the wound.

Damn. She ran into the living area and sorted through the end table. Duct tape in hand, she returned to the bathroom and adhered the tissue to her neck. With only one remaining bandage in the box, she needed it for after she dressed. The silver adhesive wouldn't be attached long enough to tear her skin.

Hair not drying fast enough, she fluffed it and wrapped the locks into a loose knot at the nape of her neck. Semi-damp curls escaped and rested on her shoulders. A quick application of limited make-up and she was ready for the dress. She went into the kitchen, removed the teabag from the mug and sipped the now cool beverage as she glanced at the garb. Black. Good. Dark and sophisticated made the evening gown an outstanding choice. Phoenix had excellent taste.

She put the teacup on top of her sketchbook on the bedside table and held the garment in front of her. The lightweight cotton and silk dress flowed beyond her knees. The long sleeves would keep her warm in the walk from the guest house to the main building. Square-shaped, the bodice was different. She loosened the towel and slipped on her undergarments. Careful to avoid the tissue, she tugged the dress into place. Snug in the bodice and hips, the gown was loose in the waist. If the dress was too tight she'd wear a shawl, but in order to find out she had to see.

Climbing onto the vanity stool, she twisted for a side view. Three rapid knocks sounded on the wooden door. The bench wobbled as she stepped down. She snuck a peek at the time as she ran past the clock. Damn, she was late. Smoothing her hair, she tugged the latch.

On her stoop was Dane weaving his fingers through his light brown, perfectly highlighted hair.

"Ready? We're waiting," he said, slightly impatient. He assessed her from the top of her head to her feet, and then narrowed his gaze on her neck. "What is that?"

The wound. How long until it would stop seeping and heal? For the past two days she'd had a slight fever, and that scared her. She pulled at the black dress, trying to loosen it from her breast area. Her belly ached.

If only she could say no to going to dinner. Impossible. She owed Dane too much and couldn't let him down.

"Can't seem to stop the bleeding." She tugged the tape. "I only have one bandage left. I'll have to change it out. Dane, I'm not--"

"I guess you'll have to wear a scarf. Your dinner date is a plastic surgeon, and it wouldn't be good for him to see a bloody neck during the lamb." Dane Bushard didn't like to have his plans altered in the least.

"Too late. What happened?" Dr. Devon Buckley moved around Dane, and with a sharp gaze focused on her neck, making her more aware of her delicate situation.

Chapter 13

Mary glanced at Dane, who shrugged as if to say the gig was up. He certainly wasn't like Phoenix, who would have rebelled and thrown the guy out.

"Knife wound from an ex-boyfriend. Dane provided me a sanctuary." She whipped her fingers to the injury, as if the flesh would magically knit back together and the gash would disappear. Wishes never grew old.

"Let me look," Devon requested, kindness in his tone.

Heart fluttering, she took a step away from the entrance, and he walked inside.

"Let's go into a better light. Bathroom?" Devon asked.

"Fine." She led the way. Humid air slowly dispensed from the bathroom. "Not enough room for three."

"I'll leave," Dane said, but held steady at the door. Periodically he'd glance at his watch. His dinner guests were anxiously waiting for his return, she was sure. She'd slap a new bandage on the cut, and they could join the group.

Enormous pain cut through her as she peeled the bandage. Feathery bits of new skin tissue stuck to the tape. Drawing a sharp breath of air, she considered jerking the adhesive to be done with it.

Devon put his fingers on top of her hand. "Wait, let me wash my hands and I'll get the bandage off. Do you have any bleach or peroxide?"

"Kitchen," she replied.

He strode from the room. Moments later cupboards opened and shut, then the faucet ran.

"I'm sorry, Dane," she said. "Do you want to leave?"

"I'll wait," he answered and shifted to the side so Devon could reenter the small bathroom.

Devon gently pulled the tape. "Relax, Mary, this is the worst part. I promise. Breathe in and out, nice and easy for me."

The scent of cleanser, dish detergent she thought, came from his fingers and stung her nose. Pain, burning pain, increased as he stripped the adhesive back. "Duct tape on the skin is never a good idea."

"Okay." Her air came out in a whoosh as she squeezed her eyes tight and tried to do the breathing as he'd instructed. With each peeled edge of tape that lifted away, she could feel a layer of precious scar tissue being ripped right along with it.

Once the dressing was removed, he probed and pried until tears stung her eyes.

"I'm going to ask you to go to my office, and we'll open this up. You've got an infection and something green, darker than pus, is under the skin. Who did the work on this?" He sounded disgusted and concerned at the same time.

Mary glanced at Dane's reflection in the mirror. His stare was straightforward. She hadn't a clue if she should say something or not. Gaze lowered, she chewed on her lip, stalling for time.

"Let's go into the living room, it's a bit cramped in here." Devon handed her a clean, dry washcloth, which she pressed to the wound. They all trooped out. Dane stood in front of the entrance, itching to exit, she was sure. Mary sat on the sofa and Devon went into the kitchen.

"Mary can't go to a doctor's office. Her ex is involved with the police and they are waiting and watching all medical facilities for her." Dane's words were solid and didn't leave room for any contradiction.

Devon went to the sink, washed his hands, turned to lean against the counter and stared at them. "Then we'll do it here."

"What?" she squeaked. She lost control of her fingers, and they jerked against the wound, reigniting the burn.

"Dane, you can go back to your party. Mary and I won't be joining you." Devon dismissed him. Devon's jacket flipped back as he drove his hands into his pockets. Whatever he jingled was the only sound in the room. The *ting ting ting* didn't relax her churning stomach or rapid heartbeat though.

"My business revolves, mostly, around the ski resort and spa twenty miles away," Devon said. "I also provide medical care of some of our residents. That being said, I have medical supplies in my car at all times. I'm going to go and get my bag and a few other items. You change out of this dress and into something unrestricting. Leave your shoulders bare, so I'll have access to your neck. I will need to thoroughly cleanse that wound. Cover with a fresh sheet or something. Do you have any allergies?" He strode to the door and held it open.

Dane held his finger and thumb in telephone speak. "Call if you need anything."

"No allergies."

Devon nodded and followed Dane.

The door shut, and shivers ran through her. She wasn't sure if it was a result of the cold air, or due to the fever. Regardless, she'd finally get the problem taken care of and eliminate the constant pain. She didn't know this man, other than he purchased flowers a couple of times a week, and his son was a college freshman. Dane must trust him or he would have spoken.

Mary left her strapless bra in place, but changed the dress for jeans. She fetched a new towel from the cupboard to wrap around her upper body. What if the infection was too far gone and she'd have a huge hole in her neck?

Where would he perform this cleaning and redressing? How would he do it? She hoped to God he'd shoot her with a numbing agent. The snap of knuckles hitting wood brought her out of the introspection. "Come in."

Devon entered, carrying a traditional style medical bag. Quaint and customary, from what she could tell, just like the man carrying the satchel.

"I'll need you to get a blanket and lay it across the kitchen bar, then lie down while I'm setting out the supplies." He laid a white cloth, taken from inside his carrier, on the counter and set metal instruments wrapped in a green material on top.

"I'm going to give you a local anesthetic. You'll have to remain very still, as the cut is close to the carotid artery, a delicate location. You were very lucky you didn't bleed out when you were attacked."

She swallowed. Anesthetic! Was he talking about cutting her open? Surgery? Lightheaded, she started to go into the bedroom for a blanket. She swayed. Devon slid placed an arm around her waist, steadying her.

He guided her to a kitchen stool. "I'll get the cloth."

A moment later, he put the green, blue and cream lap blanket from the end of the bed on the bar. He collected the two end table lamps, removed the shades and placed them near the counter. "Let me wash and we'll get started."

Mary situated herself on the newly constructed surgery slab, straightened the material underneath and bent her knees at the edge. As she gripped the sides, a rivulet of blood dripped down her neck. She closed her eyes and waited.

Water ran for several minutes.

Her breath caught. Cripes, her life had become a chaotic mess. Her grandfather was right. She shouldn't be trusted in making a decision regarding her own future, and certainly not another being's. Celibate and alone, that was her outlook. The snap of rubber brought her back to the present mess. She just wanted to get this over with and hope for a new day, which she was sure would also be a subsequent mess. She opened her eyes.

"I'm going to outline what will take place so you won't be surprised," Devon said. "The procedure will sting, but I promise you, I'll fix the problem and you'll be as good as new. I'm going to use betadine to scrub and cleanse the area. Next I'll give you a local to numb the skin. Then I'll cut through the injury and clean out the infection and stitch it together." He met her gaze. "I'll need your consent to do this procedure."

"Yes, I give you my permission to fix my neck."

He swiped a cold cloth over the wound. The scent of rubbing alcohol mixed with the plastic from gloves, filtered into the air. A packet ripped open. Soothing cold touched her skin. "I'm very good at my job and this shouldn't take but a few minutes. However, you must remain still at all times. Understand?"

"Okay." She shut her eyes as a pinprick entered. The muscles in her neck numbed a few minutes later. Metal against metal clanged a few inches away.

Pressure on her neck didn't hurt, but the thought of a blade going into her skin brought the memories of Conrad's fingers wielding the knife, trying to kill her. Her stomach muscles tightened as she felt the plastic gloved fingers touching the wound. Short, shallow breaths rushed out. Her hands fisted at her sides.

"You're knuckles are white. Do you feel my fingers?"

"No pain. I'm just remembering the attack. I'm a little scared, that's all." She breathed deep and exhaled a long string of wind.

His hand rested on her shoulder. "Deidre, my wife, was attacked at a convenience store."

She opened her eyes and instantly shut them as she saw the glint of a scalpel coming closer. "What happened?"

"No talking from this point until I'm finished. I don't want any muscles moving." He tapped her shoulder.

Pressure again, and more leakage than before dripped along her neck.

"Three years ago, she stopped to pick up a gallon of milk. We went through a lot of cow's juice at our house with an active teenager." Her skin moved, jiggled, and she felt gentle probing. "Two men, without masks, held the clerk at gunpoint as my wife walked in. She immediately pivoted to run. They shot her in the back."

Tears leaked a path from her eyes into her hair line.

"From what I understand, it's not something you ever get over. Being attacked. The pain will lessen and you'll tend to be more aware of your surroundings than you were prior to the assault, but you'll never forget."

She blinked, trying to loosen the water hanging at the edges of her eyes. Burning pain from the blade drove into her and she jerked.

The heat dissipated. "Can you feel that?"

She looked at him. "Yes," she whispered.

He held a bloody knife in his hand. "You've got a pus pocket or something dark green inside. I'll need to go deep to get it all removed. Maybe I should call an anesthesiologist to put you out?"

He glanced around the room, as if evaluating the possibility of it becoming a more equipped surgery center.

Her heart thumped against her rib cage, hard enough surely the sound became external. "No. You can't."

"Why?" He pierced her with a glance.

"There is a slim chance I'm pregnant." She licked her lips and closed her eyes, so she wouldn't see the blood on the scalpel. "I'll be fine. I won't move or jerk, I promise."

Difficult, but necessary, she unclenched her hands and gripped the edge of the counter. Could she be pregnant? She had a slight likelihood and oh what joy if she had conceived, especially if she was with child by a wonderfully kind and considerate man. Fresh tears burned her eyes. John was thoughtful and loveable, even if his goal was to catch Conrad or pry into her past.

"Well. The plot thickens. I'll remove the infection, sew the wound and then take a blood sample. Don't worry, I'll run the test myself in my lab." Cold metal of an instrument piercing her skin chilled her. "If positive, I can start you on vitamins, but I recommend you seek an obstetrician. As you've noticed, our community doesn't have a lot of babies."

She squeezed her eyes tight, trying to take herself away from the pain, willing her mind to ride the water in the Wave Pool, which was relaxing. An exhalation later, she dug her fingernails into the edge of the table and felt John's body on hers. The chlorinated liquid made a slick mask between them. John's body pressed hers into the cement handrail as the momentum of the waves picked up. He'd been aroused--she'd felt his erection against her--until she'd made the nasty comment about the cold liquid. Her stomach roiled at the memory. She'd been trying to deny the attraction. Maybe in the back of her mind she'd anticipated his betrayal.

Metal clanked, bringing her into the present. "Welcome back. I'm going to cleanse the area and sew it shut. Just a few more minutes, and you will be done. You did very well."

She blinked.

"You're very good under stress. Must be why you survived. When did it happen? I'd say almost four weeks ago."

She blinked.

"You feel a little warm, and because of the infection I'm going to start you on a safe antibiotic."

Out of the corner of her eye, she witnessed black thread going away from her face and then coming closer.

"You're going to be tired. I want you to sleep the rest of the night. I hear your stomach growling, and maybe in a while I'll let you have broth, but nothing solid for a few hours."

She blinked.

"Do you mind if I stay here tonight? I want to make sure everything goes well."

She blinked.

"Good. There we go."

She felt a firm tug and then the snick of scissors.

"Let me get the area around the wound cleaned and covered."

She grabbed his hand. "Can I see it?"

"I know you want to, but right now it's a little swollen from the probing and the black stitches stand out. I suggest waiting until tomorrow."

She blinked and turned her hand so their palms were together.

Devon smiled, a slow-growing sad smile. "Don't worry. Your secret is safe with me."

"Thank you."

A wet washcloth soothed her neck. He moved the cloth to her shoulder and wiped a few strands of hair. She closed her eyes again, wishing Conrad hadn't wanted her dead. Metal clanged and material swished. The rustling of paper brought her eyes open. He secured a bandage.

She swung her legs to the side.

"Let me help you." Arm wrapped around her waist, he accompanied her while she lowered to her feet to the floor. They slowly made their way to the bedroom.

She was tired. Dead tired. She removed her jeans and dropped the towel. He grabbed the quilt and held it up. Mary crawled underneath, between the cold sheets and sighed.

"I'll need to poke you one more time."

She stuck out her arm, knocking the empty tea cup and sketchbook off the table. "Take all you need. I'm going to sleep."

The cold sting didn't bother her, the prick and extraction of the needle wasn't a problem. Sticky Band-Aid in place, she turned to her side and tucked her arm under the blankets. What if?

"Call out if you need anything."

"'Kay." Despite how tired she was, her mind whirled with the anticipation. Should she get a home test kit to see if she was pregnant? She hadn't considered the possibility until drugs were mentioned. John wasn't on her donor list. They'd made love. Difficult to admit, but she'd fallen for John. Was Wang his real name? If his parents were Japanese and Polynesian, the Wang was an unlikely family name. He'd probably created the last name for undercover investigative work. Regardless, she couldn't reach him to tell him of an impending fatherhood, if it were true.

Mary flipped over, wanting so desperately to sleep. She sought a focal point, a boring little something to make her mind relax. Devon had stretched out on the sofa with a knitted multicolored blanket covering his legs. He held her sketchbook and would soon discover her holiday floral designs and a drawing of John. Why had she created it? John's likeness would be a constant reminder that she wasn't meant to be part of a couple. She'd always remain a single.

Her neck ached. The local must be wearing off. Should she request a pain reliever, or hope for the f'ing Sand Man to take her away from the horrible nightmare of her ex-boyfriend trying to kill her, and her counterfeit lover having saved her life?

She missed her friends, her house and to some extent, her grandfather. *Think about anything but people.* Snowflakes came to mind. She'd created a few simple metal webbed ornaments. Using Dane's workshop, she'd crafted little jeweled webbed bits of lace to hang in the store window. Would she be able to take them in tomorrow? She'd call Tim and see if he'd pick her up instead of using the bicycle. Maybe he'd be willing to cut some of the vines from the grape arbor. A sliced throat was restricting and debilitating. Surely she could play the sick card.

* * * *

John tightened his belt. He'd lost weight in the past three weeks. Not because he'd intended to shed some pounds, rather he'd lost his appetite. He told himself not to worry; obviously Mary was a survivor.

The unwrinkled sheets on the bed reflected in the hotel room mirror as he secured his shoulder holster and gun into place. He wiggled his arm into his jacket. *She's a Maniac* ring tone sounded from his phone. Debbie. Arm secure in the sleeve, he whipped the cell out of the holster.

"Yeah."

"Don't sound so pleasant. I've news," she purred.

His stomach knotted and his heart raced. Mary had to be alive. "You found her?"

"I visited Peabody in his cell, and he told me where to find Waterman. The cops and I went to his hideout in South Carolina, but he'd vacated the premises."

"Which means he's going for Mary. Fuck. Peabody probably knows where Mary's at and is playing both sides." Their jewel thief was on the move. John had to determine the probability of Waterman's destination, arrive before he did and apprehend the bastard.

"You mean if she survived," Debbie said.

His heart jerked. "She did."

"Not known at this time. However, one of her BFFs just took a piece of luggage and a large box from your girlfriend's house. Looks like she going to be seeing someone special real soon. License plate *Bushard Two*." Debbie made a kissing noise on the phone. "See you. I assume you'll be following Phoenix Bushard. I'll be tracking Waterman. Just keep in touch."

Debbie clicked off the call before John could say thanks.

Not uncommon in an investigation, he changed his plans. He had limited information regarding Mary's friends. Having arrived in South Carolina last night, he'd planned to visit with them today. As much as he wanted to track Bushard on his own, he needed help. Two beeps later, he'd connected with a colleague at the local police force. "Dan, I need a favor."

As John explained the need to have a car follow Bushard's vehicle, he clicked through documents on the computer, trying to determine any secondary houses or other associations where Mary could be stashed. Phoenix had one brother, living in Vermont.

"Thanks, Dan. I appreciate your help with this."

"Not an issue. We're here to help law abiding citizens in whatever capacity." Dan's voice was overridden by the blast of a piercing bell. A moment later, the alarm ceased. "Let me know if you need anything else." He ended the call. John threw a shirt, jeans, boxers, a sweatshirt with his old police unit's palm tree emblem, boots and necessities into a duffle. He quickly packed his computer and what he'd dubbed miscellaneous spy gear into a satchel and headed out the door.

Phoenix, driving a silver blue Ford hybrid, had just gotten onto Interstate 79 when John got behind her.

Several hours later when Phoenix drove north on 88, John confirmed her destination. Her GPS device must be on the fritz because she got lost twice and ran into construction zones a number of other times. Finally, she pulled off the current highway and onto Ninety-Second Street in New York, Upper East Side, and then into a Marriott Hotel parking lot. He found a parking spot in the garage and rushed into the hotel. Standing behind her at the registration desk, he blatantly eavesdropped until he discovered her room number. She pivoted, gave him a small smile, and walked to the elevators.

John requested a room as close to her as possible. The acne riddled, sun-damaged clerk gave him a sly smile. He could think whatever thoughts he wanted. John simply planned to find out where the girl was going.

The suite was next door to hers and outrageously overpriced, but he settled in for the night. His empty stomach gurgled with renewed hunger pangs. For the past three weeks he hadn't an appetite, yet suddenly he was famished. Excitement created hunger in him. He was on the right path to find Mary.

He considered opening the room service menu to evaluate the choices, when a quiet murmur came from the other side of the wall. She talked softly. He dug through his spy gear and drew out an audio amplifier, hoping the battery was charged. The superpower microphone adhered to the wall. John plopped the earphones in place and flipped on the device.

"Dane, I'm sorry. I'm glad you found another woman to be your eighth. I'm tired and shaky. The drive wasn't easy, lots of construction." Her tone grew weaker. "I'll look forward to meeting the plastic surgeon later in the week."

John shifted three feet and placed the microphone to the plasterboard.

"I'll be there first thing in the morning, I promise." A pause. "I'm going downstairs to get a drink and sandwich and then off to bed." She murmured, "I love you, too."

John turned off the amplifier, tucked it into the bag and threw on his jacket. He strode from the room. Avoiding the click of the latch, he inched the exit open enough to slide through and descended the staircase.

He was on a bar stool, with a dark beer in front of him when she arrived. Her light brown hair had been secured in a clip and a frown had replaced the smile she'd shared earlier. She took the first seat closest to the door, spoke softly to the bartender, and drew her cell out of the large square leather bag.

The scent of stale beer and fried foods took him back to his college days at the village bar, pleasant memories of uncomplicated times. While sneaking peeks at Bushard, he reviewed the faux leather encased menu and tapped the condensation on the drinking glass setting in front of him.

"Are you ready to order?" The waitress-slash-bartender's ponytail bounced against her shoulders as she jerked to a stop. In contrast to her unlined youthful face, her voice was gruff and no-nonsense, as if she intended to complete the order and be done with him for a few minutes.

Without glancing at her, he gave his order. "Salad, grilled chicken and a glass of water, please."

Bushard texted, talked, and finally stowed the device in her bag. She had an appetite to match any guy. Their food arrived at the same time, and her burger and fries disappeared in seconds. Bartender Tedette, according to her badge, served her another clear beverage.

John flagged Tedette, circled with his finger and after her nod, moved to the seat next to his quarry. "Hi, I'm John."

Without looking at him, Bushard withdrew her wallet, threw down two bills and stood. "I'm not interested."

"Here you are, dark beer and a gin and tonic." The gruff-voiced Tedette plopped the glasses on the table top.

Bushard strutted out of the bar.

"I'll take my bill." John nodded to his half-eaten dinner.

Tedette returned a few seconds later and handed him a slip of paper. A by-your-glance at the total, and he gave her two twenties. "Keep the change."

Chapter 14

"Who the hell are you?" The screech brought Mary upright.

Bone hit wood. "Damn." Devon cursed.

She jerked the quilt off the bed and ran to the threshold, holding the material to her chest. Phoenix stood in front of the open guest house door, staring daggers at Devon.

He hopped on one foot. His blood-stained white shirt bunched on the end of the sofa stood out, pearl against the dark blue. "Dr. Devon Buckley, and you are?"

"My best friend," Mary whispered, trying to get her sore throat to work.

"Phoenix Bushard."

"Really? Dane's sister?" he growled. Sweeping north to south, he evaluated Phoenix with a skeptical look. He put his foot on the floor and limped into the kitchen. Mary had known Devon for three weeks and never once had she heard him raise his voice. Not even when Tim had dropped the Austrian Pine on Devon's left shin.

"Yes. Where are you going?" Phoenix's no-nonsense tone should have brought Devon around. Instead, he opened the refrigerator door. The early morning sun made his silver and white hair sparkle. Sometime during the night, Devon had removed his pants. His thighs were well muscled and his rear was underwear model perfect. No shirt, no trousers and a hot body should have brought Phoenix to her knees. Instead she glared.

Mary glanced at the clock. Not early morning. Rather late, past noon. "Relax, Phoenix. Doesn't he resemble Tom Cruise with boxers and socks? Hand the man a microphone and we'll get a show." Both of them gave her dirty looks. She wanted to return to bed and roll underneath the covers. "Shut the door. It's cold."

"Where's the coffee?" Devon asked.

"I don't drink the stuff." Apparently the show wouldn't continue, so Mary tumbled onto the bed and burrowed beneath the quilt. Her neck really hurt.

The fridge door squeaked shut. Phoenix must have closed the front door, as the chilled air didn't fly around the room anymore.

Fingers touched the top of her head. "Mary?"

She folded the quilt and looked at Devon. He'd put on a t-shirt. "My throat hurts."

"What's wrong? What's happened?" Phoenix rushed to the bed, booting Devon away. "My God, Mary, what has happened?"

Mary swallowed, tears threatening to spill. Her stomach gnawed, grinding against her muscles, her heart hurt, and she wanted a pain reliever. On a sob she said, "I'm so glad you're here."

Phoenix reached for the bandage.

With gentleness, Devon pulled Phoenix's hand back. "Her ex-boyfriend cut her."

Phoenix sucked air, the noise hissing through the small space. "Conrad. That monster, I'm going to…"

Tears pricked Mary's eyes at the reminder of how much her friends cared and what an idiot she'd been to trust a man. Mary moved her arm to her stomach and bit her lip to hold the sobs at bay.

"Look, you're getting her upset." Devon scooted Phoenix to the side and touched Mary's forehead. "Mary, do you need something for pain?"

She nodded. Her stomach growled loudly in the silence.

"And something to eat?"

She nodded.

"Good. Phoenix and I will run to a restaurant and bring you something hot. First, I want to take a look at the incision." Devon used his hip to push Phoenix farther away and turned on the bedside lamp.

Phoenix frowned. Her mouth opened. A refusal would be forthcoming. Mary could feel it, along with her skin being pulled as Devon tugged the bandage, increasing the pain. He probed the area and then walked away, carrying a blood spotted scrap of white.

"Thank you. I appreciate your care. Phoenix knows what I like." Mary glanced at her friend, who stood, horror struck. The wound must be frightening. "I need to use the restroom. Are you guys leaving?"

Phoenix's hands shook as she crossed her arms, folding her coat closer. Red lining underneath the dark blue poked out. The scent of outdoor cold had been agitated by the movement and filtered into the space.

Cripes. She had to see the cut.

Devon returned with bag in hand. "Yes. First, I'm going to clean this a little. We'll let the wound get some air while I'm gone. Don't let it get wet." He touched a cold cotton swab to the injury. Spots of blood were all over the material when he lifted it.

She closed her eyes and more drops of tears fell from the edges. Wood squeaked as feet shifted. Phoenix's vanilla raspberry scent filtered into her nostrils as the mattress tilted and a soft hand touched her face. "You're hot."

Mary looked at her. Tears were in Phoenix's eyes.

She took her friend's hand, trying to keep a positive spin. "I'm sure it looks bad, but at least I had an out-clause."

"Dane never told me you were hurt," Phoenix whispered. She dropped Mary's hand, rose from the bed, and turned away. "We thought it wouldn't draw attention if I came to visit my brother." She used the back of her hand to wipe her face. "I brought some of your things."

"Phoenix," Devon said. He had wistfulness to his voice, and shifted on the bed, turning away, facing Phoenix.

Her mother hen hurried into the bathroom. Water ran, making Mary's already full bladder beg for release.

An odor, much like the iodine her mother had used on childhood injuries like scraped knees, became stronger. "Mary, this is going to sting a little, but it'll clean the area and make sure we've gotten all of the bacteria removed," Devon said.

"All right."

She didn't close her eyes, instead watched him wipe the wound and apply the topical antibiotic. At least it wasn't the old dead pumpkin color. She didn't feel the skin ripping pain she'd expected, only the cold wetness of the ointment. Probably because her bladder and empty stomach were waging war inside, taking her attention away from the immediate threat.

He removed the swab and leaned back.

Devon was gentle, kind, and had had a significant loss in the past. Her only single friend, Phoenix, would be a good mate for him. Did he purchase flowers each week in memory of his wife? Was he still grieving? She could help Devon overcome the grief and needed to be loved by a good man. Could they be matched?

"That should do it for now."

The bathroom door opened. Mary had a strong urge to crane her neck and look at Phoenix. Was she red-eyed? Had Mary caused her to cry?

"You okay?" Devon asked.

His focus was on Phoenix. She must have nodded, as he relaxed his tight shoulders.

"I need to use the facilities." Mary nodded to the powder room.

"I'll help her," Phoenix insisted.

"I can get myself to the bathroom. I'm fine." Mary slid her legs off the side of the bed.

"Any dizziness?" he asked.

"No, I'm good." Mary slowly rose. "I'm hungry, though. That broth during the night wasn't filling."

"Mary, let me help you." Phoenix's fruity scent came near. She knelt at the side of the bed. "Are you really all right?"

"Yep. Right as rain. Please go. I don't want grits and sorghum. Nasty tasting fake syrup." She waved them away. "Go. I'll be fine. Just a little nip and tuck. Devon, I might be back in ten years to have a little more work done."

Phoenix rose, like the mythological bird changed from sad ashes into a glorious radiance, becoming a strong woman. "I'll help you get there. If you're okay, then we'll leave."

They shuffled to the powder room. "Phoenix, I'm fine. Go, get me something to eat."

"I should stay."

"It's just a little scratch. Go."

"Green tea and milk too, please, I'm out." Mary stood in front of the mirror, white knuckles gripping the sink.

Devon had dressed, sans bloodied shirt, and stood waiting at the door. He'd buttoned his cashmere overcoat so only a piece of white undershirt showed beneath.

"See you in a few. Do I need to remind you to get into the bed and stay?" He tugged the knob of the entrance. Phoenix pulled in her plumes and strutted through the opening.

"Nope. Understood." Mary breathed a little easier as she heard them bickering on their way down the path. After satisfying her bladder, she glanced in the mirror to evaluate her wound while she washed her hands. The reflection had never lied to her. When she'd been a teen wanting to see boobs, they'd appeared.

She'd begged for her deceased mother to be in the reflection with her, but she hadn't appeared. Now, standing in front of the glass, she saw the knife cut. Devon was a miracle worker. Instead of jagged edges and a bump, she had a smooth, red, surface with tiny, perfect stitches. Without a doubt, in a few weeks only a small white line would appear.

She sighed. He had helped her. Until now, each time she'd looked into the mirror she hadn't seen an injury, but a murder attempt from a man she'd thought she loved. Due to the old bumpy scar she never forgot the pain of betrayal, and now that it was minute, almost disappearing along with her past, she could move forward.

Mary ran a comb through her hair, trying to unknot the strands that he'd cleaned. She changed out of the bra and removed her panties. Back in the bedroom, she searched through the drawers and found a pink tank top and matching boxers. The refrigerator beckoned--she'd have a snack, or maybe start some hot chocolate. She grasped the handle and tugged. The vial of crimson stared at her. In perfect print, *Mary's* was written on it and nothing else. Despite the urge to grab the cheese and fruit platter, she shut the door.

Pregnancy was a possibility, and in consideration she had to feed her stomach. She removed a packet of hot chocolate from the canister, rinsed the tea kettle, filled it with water and lit the gas burner. While the water heated, she removed a banana from the tiny wooden tree on the countertop.

She glanced around the cottage as she peeled back the skin of the fruit. Taking a bite from the top the banana, she waited for the water to boil. The layout of the house was perfect. A small foyer marked by bricks, then an eight-by-eight foot living area opened into the kitchen. Granite counter tops had two stools, in compensation for a table. The bedroom was sectioned off by two interior walls. A dwarf-sized door shielded the space from prying eyes. A guest could lie in bed, and if the television was positioned correctly, watch TV. Queen sized, the mattress took most of the space, but an upholstered dark blue chair held residence in the corner. One side table and a chifferobe stood along the long wall. The entire house was done in earth tones: browns, gold, oranges and blues.

Water boiled, sending off a piercing whistle. She dropped the half-eaten banana in the waste basket, turned off the burner and moved the kettle to a cool one. Ready to tear the packet, she halted. Cocoa equaled caffeine. Instant beverage forgotten, she grabbed a bottled water from the counter top. Walking through the living area, she snatched her sketchbook from the floor and entered the bedroom to collapse on the bed. Exhausted from that insignificant jaunt, she mentally added vitamins to her *purchase* list.

Covering her bent legs with the white cotton blanket, she propped the sketchpad on her lap. She reached for a pencil on the bedside table, clicked the switch on the lamp, and flipped open the hard cardboard surface. Busy fingers meant she wouldn't be reaching to touch the wound to feel the contours, the threads, the reminder about life and how quickly one could be ended.

Her hand worked the pencil on its own, without clear thought, sketching an intricate angel. Beautiful in its simple glory of gossamer wings, tiny touches of ice to the pointed ends of the wings would be a nice touch. The face was heart-shaped without detailed features. A bell skirt lay in waves around her ankles. Mary drew a rod extending from the underskirt. She drafted an equally striking male angel with mesh wings formed by thick scrolls, a strong face with a firm jaw, and attached a pole to his outstretched hand. They would be quite attractive in a floral arrangement, vase or planter.

Chilled air alerted her. She must have fallen asleep, as over more than an hour had passed. Chatter from her friends, one new and one old drew closer.

"Hey, how are you doing?" Phoenix, poised at the end of the bed, had flaming cheeks and equally scarlet lips.

Mary glanced into the living area, where Devon placed bags and a beverage carry tray on the coffee table. His entire face was red. Hmm. Something was amiss.

A flash of romance tickled her heart. Mary smiled, calculating rendezvous in her mind. "Great. I'm starving. What have you been doing?"

"We stopped by Devon's office to get you vitamins and antibiotics." Phoenix dropped her black overcoat onto the barrel chair. "You'll need to eat first."

Mary followed Phoenix's glance into the living room. Devon must have taken the bags and moved to the kitchen. "Devon?"

Phoenix tilted her head as if the question wasn't one at all.

"He got pregnancy vitamins. Did get your groove on after two nights?" Her voice rose at the end, indicating an unlikely possibility.

"Don't know if I am. I'd love to be."

Dishes rattled as Devon came into the room. "Here you go, semi-hot breakfast. Scrambled eggs, toast and yogurt."

"They didn't have a small container of milk, but I did get green tea. I'll get it for you." Cheeks pink, Phoenix rushed from the room.

Mary slipped the sketchbook to the side and took the tray from Devon. The pungent odor of eggs and slight burnt aroma from the toast made her stomach churn and nauseous at the same time. "Thanks, Devon, for everything."

"You're welcome." His face wasn't as red as earlier. He dug into his pockets and withdrew two plastic containers. "We went to my office and then to a drugstore. I got antibiotics and vitamins. I obtained the prenatal ones. Pregnant or not, the iron will aid in carrying oxygen to help rebuild the skin. The folic acid and calcium are excellent also. There's only a month's worth here, so if you are pregnant, we need to find an OB for you. I'll see if any of my friends are in the region. If not--"

"Here you go." Phoenix stopped short. "Am I interrupting anything?"

Her face lost all color. She carefully placed the cup on the side table and dropped to the edge of the bed. "You're not pregnant by him, are you?"

"No." Mary's response was echoed by Devon's.

Ah, hah. There was a spark of tenderness in the air between Devon and Phoenix.

In order to keep quiet, Mary shoved food into her mouth. She didn't want to discuss John in this forum and didn't plan to talk about pregnancy until she found out if she was positive or negative. The crunch of toast as she bit off a piece could probably be heard by Dane in the main house.

"Devon, will you help me bring in the boxes from the car?" Phoenix asked.

"Sure."

Coats in place, they left in a wave of silence. Mary took a taste of the egg. Tasty, but she preferred no yolk. She opened the sealed plastic container and sniffed. Blueberry yogurt. She took a hearty spoonful, to find it was homemade. The cool, smooth fruit embedded in cream slid down her throat. Perfect. Soon the treat was gone, but the fresh scent of blueberries remained in the air.

Mary took the tray to the kitchen, dumped the remains down the disposal and got rid of the trash. Her teeth felt fuzzy. Back in the bathroom, she brushed away the slimy covering, adding mint to the blueberry. Red and swollen, the black Xs of the stitches stood out on her skin. She glanced at the pill bottles on the side table. Deciding to take a vitamin and one of the antibiotics, she struggled with the caps and then downed the tablets with a significant amount of lukewarm honey-sweetened green tea.

Under the covers again, she brought her sketchbook onto her lap. What was taking Phoenix and Devon so long? As she flipped to the angel drawing, the door opened.

A suitcase landed on the bottom of her bed, and a large box on the floor at the end. "Here is a large box of band aids, so you won't have any reason to use duct tape again." He smiled.

Mary shoved the sketch to the side and leaned forward. "Thanks. What else did you bring me?"

"Winter clothes. Thought they'd be important. A lightweight jacket. We'll have to purchase a winter coat for you. There was a country store in the next county. They had a nice selection. I'll unpack the stuff. Probably what you'll be most interested in is in here."

"I'm sorry, but I need to leave. I have patients to see. I'll return this evening. Mary, I took the liberty of calling Frank and telling him you wouldn't be in today." Devon held his stained white shirt in his hand and the black bag in his other.

Mary leaned on her heels. "Thank you. Did you reassure him I'd go to Mrs. Landware's tomorrow?"

A low rumble, somewhere in his chest, fought to get out. "Yes. I told him I'd take you myself."

She plopped her rear onto the mattress. "That's not necessary. You've done enough."

Phoenix removed her coat and tossed it onto the blue chair in the corner. "Who is Mrs. Landware?"

"A client of the floral shop. I'm going to decorate her house for the holidays." Mary smiled. She liked working with the plants and flowers, maybe more than jewelry design. Again, the thought of settling in Cage cemented.

"I'll take her," Phoenix announced.

"Why don't we all go together? I'll be here tomorrow at eight sharp." He pivoted and walked out the door.

"Is he always like that?" Teeth clicking on the zipper of the suitcase followed her question.

"I don't know him very well, but if I were to guess, yes, he is like that. Why don't you know these people? You've been to visit Dane before." Mary clawed a thin, long sleeved t-shirt from the suitcase.

Phoenix removed a blouse and carried it to the closet, slipped it on a hanger and repeated the action with another clothing piece. "They've only lived here for three years and I haven't been introduced to a lot of the neighbors. No, they've been here for three or four. I was supposed to attend a dinner party last night and meet everyone, but I couldn't get through some construction zones. Detours took me a long way off course." She piled a few athletic items on the side of the bed.

"While you're telling me about your attraction to Devon, will you hand me the surprises in the box?" For the first time in three weeks, hope and excitement thrilled her. She was going to be all right, and Phoenix was here.

Phoenix gaped at her. "I'm not attracted to Devon." She bent and scooted the container to the side of the bed. "This was heavy. I'm glad he dragged the box in for me."

As cardboard flaps rubbed together, Mary whispered, "But you kissed him."

Phoenix's head popped up, then she fell onto her rear. "How did you know?"

Mary chuckled and slid a t-shirt over her tank top. "Written all over both of your faces." She glanced into the box. "So you might be coming to visit me quite a bit?"

"Yes, of course I'll visit. Should I be interested in him? I don't know anything about him. Other than he's a sweet and gorgeous doctor." She hauled a metal tool chest from inside.

"Yes, you're a good match with Devon. Oh, Phoenix, you're the best friend ever. Thank you for my kit." Mary slipped her legs from the side of the bed and sat on the floor in front of the toolbox. Latches flicked and she opened the top. A touch to a button on the front released two sets of drawers. Her tools, pliers, tweezers, shears, saws and wax gleamed in the overhead light. In the bottom were her flex shaft machine, soldering devices, scales, blades and wire wrapping tools. Ring stretchers, stone grading and gem instruments as well as hammers, glues and solvents were layered. Burs, drill bits, gauges and measuring devices were in the crate on top. Missing from the valuable stash were her small screwdrivers. To confirm, she sorted through the items again.

"Something wrong?"

"Not really, just a couple of things missing. Files and small screwdrivers. I only have a couple inches of twenty-two gauge yellow gold wire and a small jump ring of white gold. I have a project and could have used a five-point-three millimeter, twenty gauge ring."

"You think Conrad took your bits and pieces."

"Maybe, or his partner." She jerked her neck to look at Phoenix, regretting the quick motion as the stitches pulled and fresh pain rippled through her neck. "Have you heard from the police? Did they get Conrad? Do you know who helped him?"

Too fast and too much agony came to her mind and affected her stomach. Mary closed the case, choked back the bile lodged in her throat and took a deep breath.

"You okay?"

"I'm a little dizzy. Guess I moved my neck too far. Please help me climb into bed." Mary held out her arm.

Phoenix latched onto Mary's bicep and threw back the cover that had been dragged to the edge with her earlier. "Here you go."

Mary fell onto the mattress and moved her legs under the sheet and blanket. "Whew. I guess that little bit of activity took some energy."

"Devon told you to rest today." Phoenix frowned and then moved the toolbox to the side and finished unloading the first carton.

"Oh, Phoenix, shoes. I wanted shoes. Thank you so much."

Phoenix touched Mary's forehead. "Your fever has reduced, despite all of your moving around. I'm going to stow this luggage in the closet and take the box out to the trash can. Then I'm going to raid Dane's fridge for some supplies and make soup for you. While I'm doing that, you are to sleep. Got it?"

"Yes, Mommy Dearest." Mary shut her eyes. She didn't want her heartbreak to affect Phoenix, who, from the blushes appearing every time Devon's name came into play, was at the edge of falling in love.

"Who is this?"

Mary pried open her eyelids and glanced toward Phoenix, who held the sketchpad.

"The donor."

Chapter 15

John knew Bushard's Vermont destination, so he didn't follow her immediately, instead chose to sleep for the first time in weeks. The next day, he contacted Debbie to verify her status and investigated Phoenix's brother.

John's tires bumped and squeaked as he navigated over the cobbled streets of the quaint hamlet of Cage. Twenty minutes later, he parked in the lot of a New England style house with a squeaking shingle on a metal chain identifying the building as *Molly's Place*. He positioned his car across the street and walked inside. A sign indicating *Find a seat* and *I'll be right with you* had been propped at the entrance.

None of the tables were open, so he took a stool at the counter. An overweight woman wearing a turban, green dress and ruffled crisp apron plopped a glass of less-than-crystal water in front of him. "What'll ya have?

"The special." He moved the glass of water. "And an Evian, if you have one."

"Liver and onions and coffee right up."

She had to be kidding. What had happened to Vermont's promotion of maple syrup? He watched her sway. Her large hips skimmed a rushing boy carrying a tray of dirty dishes. She opened the fridge and removed a clear glass bottle.

The container banged against the ceramic bar top and immediately after, she handed him a menu. He appreciated a saucy waitress, and he imagined she was quite snappy.

"We only carry local bottled water, Clear Springs. The meatloaf is good, the chicken soup is fresh, but I recommend the Swiss steak." Her narrow face didn't budge from its dour expression. She dropped her hands on her hips and tapped her fingers against the stained cloth.

"Thank you for the review, ah…"

"Princess."

"Princess." *Very difficult to say with a straight face.* He handed the menu back. "Steak and sides of your choice."

Princess strutted away, grabbing a coffee carafe along the way.

A glance around the crowded, steamy room didn't expose Waterman or Mary, although the likelihood of her being there was nil. Locals occupied the chairs, as indicated by the head nods and shouting across tables. One cop wearing a chocolate striped brown uniform chatted with a curvy blonde wearing a third of the uniform Princess sported.

A plate of food was shoved onto the silver shelf. A few clicks to his cellphone, and he brought up Mary's photo as his waitress grabbed the platter from the hot source.

"Here you go," she said, setting his order before him. "Let me know if you need anything."

"I do. Have you seen this woman?" He held out his phone, moving the face so the light wouldn't blind her.

Her eyes widened and then she lowered them to the memo pad. "No."

She wrote on the slip of paper, ripped the ticket and weighted it down with a salt shaker. Princess meandered to the end of the counter, chased the blonde away and whispered into the cop's ear. A moment later, the tree swaggered toward John.

John's attention focused on the meal in front of him. The aromas from gravy, fresh whipped potatoes and sweet corn tantalized his nostrils. A taste proved the food to be as delicious as the scents.

"Hello. I'm Sheriff Todd." He extended a hand, the fingers resembling franks.

John sighed, put down his fork, reached around his wool overcoat and into his suit jacket pocket. Handing the credentials to the cop, he waited as the man evaluated them. He believed his old police detective badge held more weight than the ACI ID.

Sheriff Todd returned the holder and took the next seat. "Okay. Who are you looking for, detective?"

John removed a twenty from his pants pocket and placed it under the salt shaker. He replaced the ID into his jacket and brought Mary's photo onto his cell.

Todd nodded, glanced around and leaned in. "Why are you looking for her?"

"She was a witness to a robbery and is in danger." John went on to explain the theft and that Andee Waterman, an armed and dangerous criminal, would be coming or was currently in the area.

Todd dropped from the stool and hiked his pants. "We'll watch out for the little lady."

John stood. "I'll take care of Keefe. You keep a look-out for Waterman. I'll have his photo emailed to your station. Confidentiality is imperative, Sheriff Todd. We don't want to spook him. I want him to return to jail."

"She works at the Garden and Floral Design Center over on Route Three. She's staying in Bushard's onWinding Way." Sheriff Todd sniffed and placed a palm on the butt of his pistol. "But you can leave. We take care of our own."

"I'm staying."

Todd nodded.

John left the cafe, surprised and pleased his plan was unfolding without little effort. He popped a stick of gum in his mouth, enjoying the fresh spearmint flavor as he entered Winding Way into his GPS. A few moments later, his stomach roiled in anxiety. He turned onto the lane leading to Three Rivers Estate. What if she…didn't want him?

Bushard's concrete drive was wide and wrapped around in a full circle. The place resembled *Wuthering Heights*, at least the one in the movie, complete with a brick path winding around the side. He smiled, remembering how he surprised his sister by agreeing to watch the extremely boring movie with her.

A white SUV was parked in a separate lane leading to the guest house. Outdoor lights lit the stones, directing him from the secondary structure to the seemingly empty main house. He parked behind a row of bushes at least two stories in height, got out of the car and took a run around the property, looking for exit points.

Stake-outs were his least favorite activity, and not having performed the mundane task in over five years, he'd forgotten how much he disliked the job. He crossed the rear portico and traipsed through a stack of pungent decaying leaves until he came in sight of the rear of the guest house. The lights clicked on, but he didn't see a shadowed outline inside. Was she at home, or had a timer been set? When he scouted the perimeter, all the windows had shades drawn, shielding the interior. John reentered his car and waited.

Time crept by. John could be wasting precious moments if Phoenix was actually here to visit her brother. No, Mary had to be here. The cop had confirmed the fact. Why else would California-born Waterman travel to Vermont, the East Coast, instead of the familiar ground of the sunny West Coast?

A few minutes later, a silver-headed man left the guest house with Phoenix trailing behind. John grabbed his binoculars and scanned the area. After the couple took items from Bushard's car, they reentered the house. An hour passed before the old guy climbed into his white SUV and drove away. John focused on the house, watching for movement, knowing Mary was within the confines.

Ground level motion detectors flashed on with a slight shifting of leaves. Branches leaned closer to the bramble surrounding the north side of the cottage. He twisted the lens and the focus zoomed on the tree line. No human life--rather a woodland creature making its way across the line of trees. The outdoor security light lining the driveway beamed, blinding his view for a moment. His eyes readjusted, and only stillness prevailed. Night fell quickly, dispelling his small gleam of hope to see Mary.

Exhausted and dismayed, John settled against the driver's seat and closed his eyes to review the data. What had he missed? Diamonds were missing and Mary had wanted his shout-out to be diamonds. Peabody had attacked her because she wouldn't tell him where the jewels were. How did Waterman pinpoint her in Vermont? Had he put an illegal tap on Mary's friends' phones? No, too much work, and he didn't appear to be a bright guy. Maybe Mary was involved in the theft. Doubt clouded his mind. Instead of approaching the house, he'd wait. Waterman would appear at some point.

Sleepy, John opened the window for fresh air. A cool breeze chilled him, but also shocked him into alert mode. The zing of his phone alerted him to a message. A couple of taps and he read Debbie's note of entering Vermont. She'd connect with him tomorrow night. After checking his mail, he dragged a bottle of water and a protein bar from his satchel.

Falling asleep was a mistake, and he awakened at five o'clock with an urgent need to piss. The cramping in his lower abdomen made him question eating the protein bar after a fat-filled meal at the diner. He used the binoculars to scout the area. Not seeing any sign of human life, he threw the magnifiers onto the seat and drove to the nearest gas station. Field work wasn't the right job for him. He'd failed.

He strode through the mini-mart to the bathrooms. Business taken care of, he used the sink faucet to freshen his face. Swiftly gathering snacks, water and super sized coffee, he paid and stuffed the items in his car, then refueled his tank. As much as he dreaded going back to surveillance mode, he didn't have an alternative. With no warrant and many contradictions rushing through his thoughts, he had to entrap.

Hours passed, making him question if he had the right place. He expected the local police to come by and check on his progress, but they hadn't, which made him even more wary. Shaded by the oncoming gray afternoon, he exited the car and took another trip around the perimeter. John stopped under the drooping branches of a fifty-year-old willow as tall as the brick flue on the roof of the house. He leaned against the bark. Sharp and rough, the wood felt good against his back. Lingering and stalking weren't things he was adept at, but he'd wait and watch to see her. Her tone trilled through the bare branches, along with a more masculine voice. Laughter, sweet feminine giggles rippled across the willow branches, bringing him fully alert. Heart palpitations thumped his chest, causing him a sharp, twisting pain. John strode from under the shade, stepped forward, and his suspicions mounted.

The old man had his arm wrapped around her waist. She giggled, not a chuckle, and not a deep throated laugh, but a flirting snigger. "Thanks for helping at Mrs. Landware's house. I think she's in love with you, like every other single female in Cage."

John swallowed and tightened his hands into fists.

"Humph. Let me get it, obviously you're unsteady this afternoon." The guy had a rusty voice. "Did you take your vitamins?"

"I will now." Her trill had a sweet escalation.

The man pulled Mary into his arms and whispered into her ear.

John whipped his gun from his shoulder holster. "Release her."

Their heads, previously tucked together, drew apart and they stared at him with eyes equal to the size of owls'.

"John," she said and promptly fainted into the dude's arms.

The fossil shoved the door with his foot.

"I've a gun leveled on your back. Let her go." John released the safety on his Glock. The only thing he knew about this guy was that he held Mary as if he wouldn't let her go.

"Drop the gun," Phoenix Bushard shouted from behind John.

A sharp twist, keeping his revolver level on the man supporting Mary, and John stared at Bushard.

"It's you." Her hand shook, making the old .32 look larger and her confidence weak. She'd never used the pistol before or she would have known to move closer, within shooting range. "Oh fuck, I led you here. Drop your gun."

He held steady. "You heard me say I had a weapon, right?"

Phoenix's jaw firmed and both hands clenched the butt of the pistol. "Yeah, but she's my best friend."

A click pierced the sudden silence. John took his gaze off Phoenix and glanced at the guest house. His woman and the man had disappeared.

Chapter 16

Mary, lying on the bed in Dane's guest house, listened to John and Devon's softly spoken words, refusing to open her eyes. The medicinal scent of antiseptic mingled with men's cologne and the tinny smell of old blood. How had John found her?

Guilt rippled through her. She should have turned in the diamonds when she'd found them packed away in the toe of her finest heels. Snug in the tip of the pointed shoe, held tight by the traveling case. Millions of dollars' worth of gems had been flaunted in the open on the cruise ship. Conrad had attacked her and from that point on, she'd forgotten about them. Easy enough to do--her only concern had been survival.

The silky evening bag encrusted with agate stones was stashed away in the tiny closet two feet from the bed. All of a sudden the investigator seeking the stolen jewels had found her. He wouldn't be fooled again. His voice sounded loud in the room, bringing her out of her contemplations. If she gave the stones to him, would he leave?

"Get away from her." John's light footsteps came closer to the side of the bed.

"I'm a physician, Dr. Devon Buckley." Devon loosened the scarf from around her neck. His cool fingers felt good on her hot skin. Could she continue to avoid the confrontation by keeping her eyes closed? Perhaps if she played possum they would all clear out, leaving her alone.

"It's been four weeks. She should have healed by now," John said.

"She would have if she had gotten treatment." Devon's voice came out gruff. Next, the bandage was removed.

She didn't think the throbbing came from her wound, rather her heart. John had found her, but had he because of their night together, or as a result of the everlasting search for the diamonds?

"Why isn't she waking up?" John's voice sounded rusty, quiet and concerned.

Devon's hand rested on her forehead. With silted eyes, she peeked at him. He winked and swiped his fingers across her face. "She underwent surgery recently. Her energy is lagging."

The mattress shifted. Devon asked, "Why are you here?

A new weight rested beside her. "Confidential."

"Get away from my friend," Phoenix piped up.

"No." Rough fingers entwined with hers. John's. "She's under protective custody. I suggest you return to South Carolina. I'll get a physician to take care of her, so you can leave as well, Dr. Buckley."

"She's my patient. I'll maintain care of her, until she awakes and tells me otherwise." Devon sat on her other side and the click of a medicine bottle being opened pierced her eardrums. "Unless you have the documents to prove you have arrest powers, I suggest you leave."

No, she didn't want him to leave. Would he? Mary stared into John's deep brown eyes. She'd only seen gentle humor in his gaze, but now fear mixed with anger seeped through. "John."

"I--" Fury personified came through that one word. He cleared his throat. "Was worried," he whispered as if they were alone in the room.

"Mary, after you eat you'll need to take the meds. I called in an order for take-out." Plastic hit the bedside table, followed by the clack of the pills. "Do you want us to leave so you can be alone with him, or do I call the sheriff?"

Mary met his gaze. "He isn't the one who attacked me, Devon. I need to talk to him."

He frowned, but tilted his head in acknowledgement. "Phoenix and I will get carry-out and return in thirty to forty minutes. I trust you won't make my patient move, Mr.--"

Mary tried to pull her fingers away. John tightened his.

"Kajiyama, John Kajiyama."

"Mr. Kajiyama, I need to have a word with you in the other room," Devon insisted. His voice thundered. She witnessed a side of the man she never knew existed, but had suspected. Not only was he honorable, but also protective of her. They were virtual strangers brought close because of fate and circumstance.

Phoenix shoved past John to stand next to the bed. John stood and walked from the room. Devon studied her where she lay on the bed. Apparently he made a decision, and followed John.

"I'm sorry, Mary. I led him to your hide-out. Do you want me to try and get a rescue together? Get you away from here?" Phoenix whispered, and flicked her fingers. As instructed, Mary rolled over. Phoenix took the pillows and fluffed them, piling an additional cushion in the front.

Repositioned, Mary sighed. "No, I'm tired of running. John will protect me."

"From your drawing, he's the father?" Phoenix never mixed her messages or tried to bury information. She always straight-out asked. "Do you want to be left alone with him? John Wang, right?"

"Yes, it's complicated." *Hold back the tears, until they all leave,* "Not your usual type. You'll tell me what happened and why he's here?" Phoenix started for the doorway. "Before Jenn finds out, because we won't get any rest once she realizes her prediction turned out to be accurate."

"Let's go, Phoenix," Devon demanded from the hall. "The food will be cold by now. Mary needs to eat."

"Later. Nothing spicy, okay?" Mary was confident she'd hurl if anything with tomato paste went down her throat.

"Got it. We'll be back in a few," Phoenix said as she left the room, and the entry door shut a moment later.

Mary's head fell against the bed rail. *Complicated* didn't touch on her situation. She stared at John as he carried a glass of water. He set the crystal on the bedside table, and then sat on the mattress.

"Let me see," he whispered. "May I?"

She nodded.

He pulled the collar of her blouse away from her neck, tucked it under and removed the bandage with such gentleness tears stung her eyes.

His frown didn't make her feel all that secure. He narrowed his eyes, adding to her unease. "Tell me, everything."

"Because you want me to be guilty of jewel theft?" Her stomach clutched in fear. What if she'd read the signs wrong? No kiss to make it better? She'd dreamed of a reunion with him because he sought her out of love. The first thing he did, in her fantasy, was to join their lips. If not her mouth, then a kiss to her cheek, forehead or even an ear would be acceptable. But like all the other men in her life, he didn't love her. Had unreasonable expectations and had used her. "Can the story wait?"

"Yes, the story can wait." His brown eyes pierced her, but he replaced the dressing and drew her blouse to cover it. A caress to her ear, then he tucked some hair behind it and stroked her cheek. Her heart rate doubled. Maybe she had finally found her prince? "I was afraid you were dead. The cut. Blood. Why'd you run from me?"

She folded the sheet, smoothed the surface and placed her hands on top. "I didn't run from you. I ran from... Did you get Conrad?"

His fingers, hovering over her cheek, dropped and he lowered his hand. To her surprise, he walked around the bed, propped the un-indented pillows against the rails and snuggled beside her. Weaving their fingers, he held hers firmly. "Yes. He'll never bother you again. I'll make certain of that."

"How is that possible?"

"I work for the Atlantic Coast Investigation firm. We were hired by your insurance company to find the diamonds."

"And you started with me? Believing I was guilty, part of a robbery scheme? Romanced me in hopes of finding the stones?" Bitterness vibrated through her with each word.

"It's more than that. Do you know who your boyfriend's partner is?" The hard edge he put on *boyfriend* was easy to ignore, but his stringent evaluation unnerved her.

"Ex-boyfriend. No. I'd never met him, or her. I'm not sure which, since I never heard him talk during the robbery." She rolled to her side to look at him. He was so very handsome. She'd tried to replicate his image on her artist pad, but had failed. No sketch could compare to the live, vibrant man holding her hand and caressing her fingers.

"What makes you think the robber was a woman?"

"The way she or he moved through the store. Fluid, delicate steps. She or he smelled like cinnamon, and I've found that men tend to buy cologne with a spicy base and women with a floral citrus base."

"So you think the partner was a man after all?"

She shook her head. "No, I think it was a woman covering her femininity with male attributes, including shoes and cologne."

* * * *

"According to the information we gathered, Peabody's partner's name is Andee Waterman, male from Detroit, Michigan. He's served many years of jail time and when I catch him it'll be decades before he gets out." John had hoped she'd tell him more, for example, why she ran. Why she obviously had an escape plan in place.

"Huh. Guess I was wrong."

It was easy to pretend to right the covers under her and move closer, pressing their joined hands between their stomachs.

"Are you okay? Want me to take you to a real doctor tomorrow?" He stroked her face. She was gorgeous and as pale as a snowflake. His heart told him to ignore the evidence and make slow love to her, but the facts of the case and his suspicions kept him grounded.

"Devon is a real doctor, and he's taken very good care of me." She wet her lips. "Are you going to arrest me or kiss me?"

"You're a bold woman, Mary Keefe." Was she guilt-free? If so, why had she run?

She flipped onto her back. "Yeah, that's me. I'm exactly as you see."

"I see a complicated, innocent woman." He'd wanted to say *Mary, I love you*, but the time wasn't right, and why would she believe him? They'd spent a few days together. Women might fall in love in such a short amount of time, but men didn't. He wanted to be her protector, and in order to appear capable of doing the job, he had to keep his true feelings to himself--for now.

"I take that to mean you're not going to take me to the cops in Keefe." She rubbed her lips together. "So, I want the sexy kind of kiss."

"Whatever my lady wants will be granted." He propped an arm on the other side of her head and stared into her beautiful green eyes.

She wrapped a hand at the back of his neck and tugged him closer. John resisted kissing her. Being ill, she should rest. Instead he lowered her hand, but their pinky fingers remained touching.

"Thank you," she mumbled.

"For what?" He was confused. Maybe she wanted to thank him for not giving her a kiss?

"For saving my life in Kingston."

"I wish you would have talked to me about getting accosted by Peabody in the hallway of the ship," he growled.

"I tried."

"You said you thought you saw an old boyfriend, not that he'd approached you."

"We're back!" Phoenix shouted from the door.

John jumped from the bed as if he was a teenager caught by the girl's parents. "That was fast. Do you want me to carry you into the living room?"

Mary didn't look at him. "No, I'll just change into sweats and be out in a minute."

John nodded. He'd probably offended her, but he had to get part of the anger off his chest. Belying his thoughts, he strode around the bed and held out a hand. She raised her liquid eyes and trustingly placed her palm against his. He drew her closer, until their chests met, and whispered, "I'm here to help you. Don't fight me. Let me do my job."

"I know." Mary stepped to the chifferobe. He drew in a deep, relaxing breath and walked into the living room.

Phoenix was busy placing food on the coffee table. He guessed by the *clunk-clunk* coming from the ice-maker, the doctor was getting ice for drinks.

He didn't miss the sneer coming from Devon's face when he turned. Something must have happened while the two were gone, because the animosity had grown thicker.

"Who exactly are you?" Devon set the glasses on a counter top and then placed his hands on his hips.

"I'm with Atlantic Coast Investigations. Fraud division. My company's been hired by Lighthouse Insurance to investigate the robbery that took place at Mary's store. I'm also a trained police officer, having worked as a detective with the Fort Myers Police Department in Florida for ten years."

"Fraud? You think she was involved, that she helped them?" Phoenix rushed the words.

"I don't."

"Are you taking her to the police?" Devon asked.

"No. She hasn't done anything to warrant an arrest. She will be under my personal protection, but we'll remain here until the thief's accomplice has been found," John responded in a calm, quiet tone.

Phoenix glanced in his direction. "You caught Conrad?"

"Yes, in Kingston. Mary doesn't need to fear him, but she must be aware the second guy is out there. Why are they so anxious to find her?" John glanced between them.

"Her grandfather was pressuring her. He had threatened to sell her parents' home unless she had a..." Phoenix's eyes glazed over with unshed tears. "She wasn't involved in the robbery. Mary would never steal anything, nor help others in illegal activities. She's very honest and trustworthy."

"Thanks, Phoenix. What's for dinner?" Mary had put red on her cheeks and lips, but she still resembled a porcelain doll.

"Chinese," Phoenix said, staring at her.

"Why are you all looking at me as if I've risen from the dead?" she asked.

"Because your color is such that you could have." Phoenix rose and pressed Mary's shoulder until she sat on the sofa.

Mary grabbed an egg roll on the way to the cushions. "Who's looking for me?"

"Andee Waterman," John replied.

"I don't know you," the doctor said. "I barely know Mary, but I do know she wouldn't take something that doesn't belong to her. She's already been attacked. If Waterman is looking for her, then we need to create a plan to keep her safe." Buckley lowered to the sofa beside Phoenix and placed a glass of milk in front of Mary.

"Stay in the house until the guy has been caught?" Phoenix suggested.

"Can't. I need to purchase gold and silver wire to make accents for Mrs. Landware's holiday decorations, and then go to a floral warehouse." Mary glanced at Buckley. "I must get branches of holly, and pine boughs from the store." She sipped from the glass of milk.

"I'm sure the kid who takes you home can deliver holly and pine to her house," Buckley said. "Make a list and Phoenix and I will go to the warehouse. I wouldn't know what to buy for gold and silver though."

Mary sighed. "The warehouse doesn't have the gauge I want. Frank will have to order it, and delivery is slow because of the holiday."

"Can the wire be ordered from the internet?" John asked.

"Yes, if I had access to my credit cards, but I'm hiding out." Mary huffed. "From you, and now Andee Waterman."

"There will be no hiding from me." John stuck his fork into her cashew chicken and stole a bite. "Can you get internet access in this godforsaken country?"

"Dane has dial-up," Phoenix said.

"There's an internet cafe in Cage. You can go there, but Mary needs to rest the remainder of today." Buckley laid down the law. "Or you might have internet access at the hotel."

"I'll be staying here. Do you have a problem with that?" He ground his teeth. What exactly was their relationship? "I'll use my phone to order the supplies."

Silence prevailed while they ate, except for the clack of chopsticks or fork tines hitting pottery, providing an ironically musical cadence. Finished with the meal, Mary slumped against the sofa cushions. Buckley and Phoenix went into the kitchen. The clang of dishes being washed mingled with their whispering.

Mary glanced at him. "John, I need to take a couple of vitamins. They're on the nightstand. Would you get them for me, please?"

"Sure." He left the room, keeping her in sight for as long as possible. Her expression sent jolts of electricity through him. Deep inside he suspected something else, outside the threat of being hunted, was shady. More than that, she'd likely she'd bolt again. At the doorway, he pivoted.

Mary scurried into the kitchen and obtained a bottle of water from the fridge. "Okay, what's all the whispering about?"

"We're not sure you'll be safe here. I need to leave the day after tomorrow. I'm sorry, fall break is over or I'd stay with you. Devon thinks you should go to his house." Phoenix bit her lip.

"No." John hadn't shouted, but the forcefulness of the word coming from his mouth made the utterance seem like he was yelling.

Chapter 17

"We need to talk!" John stage whispered, as Mary escorted Devon and Phoenix toward the guesthouse door.

Mary nodded. "Devon, Frank has an account at the wholesalers. I'll call him on my new pay-as-you-go phone." She smiled at Phoenix, who'd provided it as well as the tool kit and winter clothing. "And let you know what he says to do. If you can't find what I've written on the list, give me a jingle and I'll try to think of a substitute."

"Yes. I understand. Rest, Mary. If I see your stitches pulled tight, or your neck red and swollen, I'll be miffed." Devon folded the inventory sheet and shoved the paper into his pocket.

She choked back a sob, pasted on a small smile and nodded. John's hand rested on her hip, his lower arm at her waist, reassuring her of his strength and presence. Mary shut the door, and he secured the locks.

"Back to bed with you." He guided her the few feet to the mattress.

"I need to brush my teeth, and I'd love to have a bottle of water." She kept her gaze on the floor, not wanting to show him her insecurities.

"Sure." His light footsteps barely sounded on the wood floors as he went into the kitchen where she'd left the refreshment.

Mary used the facilities, scrubbed her blotchy face, brushed her teeth and settled on the bed. She drew the pale blue covers and was smoothing the Egyptian cotton sheet when he walked into the room. What would happen? He'd said she was innocent, but she wasn't. She'd held onto the diamonds. How could she tell him without breaking the fragile bond holding them together?

He held a laptop under his arm and extended a container of water with the other hand. "I want to try and connect."

"I thought insurance agencies didn't have advanced equipment. You seem to have super powerful devices. You're a techi with WiFi?" She took hold of the plastic and sipped the cool water.

"I've ordinary WiMAX. I can tell by your expression you don't understand." He lay beside her, his back against the white wrought iron bedrails. "WiMAX, or the Worldwide Interoperability for Microwave Access, is a wireless digital communication system. Broadband access is available up to thirty miles for fixed stations and thirty-one miles for mobile stations. Longer distance, efficient bandwidth usage and less interference. Let's see if we have a station nearby." He booted and the sweet hum of a hard drive became background music. "If not, I'll use the cell, but it will take longer."

"Nice. Try jewelry warehouse dot com." She placed the bottle on the table and leaned on her elbow to look at the screen.

A few snaps and clicks, and her favorite site flooded the screen.

"Silver and gold?" He caught her attention.

"Yes, gold over sterling silver is fine and it'll cost less."

"What gauge size?"

"I'm not sure what would work best. I'd planned to create a sample first." Feather pillows always needed plumping, so she threw her fist into the softness and then laid her face on the fat end, facing him.

"What would you typically use in your work?" He brought large gauge silver wire onto the screen.

She yawned, and then covered her mouth with her hand. "Sorry. The size varies according to the project." Another yawn slipped out. "Size ten or five."

The wire was measured by inches. "Mary?"

* * * *

John glanced at her. Mary's eyes were closed and soft, even breaths came from her slightly open mouth. He added twenty units of silver for both sizes and added it to the cart with overnight shipping.

She'd removed the bandage covering her stitches. Sliding the laptop to the table, he bent over her, evaluated her wound and was amazed that within a few hours the site already looked less swollen and red. That bastard Peabody would never get parole if John could prevent it.

He picked up the computer, requested five feet of gold-plated wire, covered, and an accessory kit to mold the stuff together. John didn't have any experience in jewelry design, but he didn't want to wake her. Better to have too much than not enough. Adding the items to the cart, he checked out and used his credit card for payment.

Mary rolled onto her side, away from him. He went into his work email account. Debbie had sent a video. Due to a weak signal, he couldn't open the link. His search revealed a message that made his stomach nauseous. *Waterman's in Vermont, near Crazy or whatever town you're located in.*

John typed a response, asking for details and reinforcements.

Only know what you know, was the reply. *We're not the police, simply investigators.* She wrote in all caps. *I'm delayed. I'll see you in a couple of days.* She signed out.

A solid hour had passed while he communicated over the net. A couple more clicks and sites visited, and he shut down the laptop. He slid from the bed, trying not to jar Mary, and replaced the sketchpad on the dresser with his computer.

It was easy enough to convince himself that snooping through her drawings could provide information about the size of the wire. He carried the booklet into the living area and flipped on a lamp. The first few pages consisted of floral arrangements. Nice, but elementary in style. Ten sheets later, he paused and his heart knocked into his ribs. His likeness had been sketched with the wave pool in the background. Grabbing a silver dish on the end table, he glanced at his reflection. Christ, when had he gotten lines around his eyes? He snapped his tongue against his teeth. She'd thought of him during the separation. He'd certainly thought of nothing but Mary and the danger surrounding her. He'd protect her life or die trying.

He put the tray down and reviewed another section of floral designs, much better than the initial ones. Finally, the best of her drawings, an angel. She'd drafted the creation from several different angles. The delicate wings, so fine they looked like spun webs of gold. Mary had a gift. Hopefully, he'd capture Waterman and she could go back to her true profession as a jewelry designer.

In all probability Mary Keefe would fight him the entire way, but he'd win. He always did, and he wasn't going to let this case be the one to ruin his record. Nor would he allow her to ditch him again as she had in Kingston. They were going to be in constant contact.

He glanced into the bedroom. She'd left the bed. Water running proved she'd gone into the bathroom. Nap time was over. He checked his watch. Seven o'clock. His appetite had returned. Tonight he'd get take out from one of the down-home restaurants. Hopefully, Waterman would be caught by the Sheriff's Department and John could pursue Mary whole-heartedly.

Two raps vibrated the entrance of the guest house. He placed the sketch pad on the coffee table and made his way to the door. At the third knock he snapped the lock. "Who is it?"

"Devon and Phoenix. What's going on?" Devon's angry tone could have punctured a hole in the portal.

Behind him the door opened. He glanced at Mary and waved his hand for her to return inside the bedroom. It was highly unlikely Waterman would simply walk into her home, but he wasn't one to take chances. As she disappeared behind the wall, he opened the vibrating door.

"What's with the cloak and dagger routine?" Phoenix asked as she barged into the room, carrying several plastic bags filled with greenery.

Devon dropped the large box on the floor and stood, white knuckled hands fisted at his sides. "Mary?"

She slid across the threshold. She'd applied make-up, but the pink on her lips made her face appear all the whiter.

"Damn, you look dreadful. You need to crawl back into bed," Phoenix insisted.

"I'm concerned." Devon snapped his cellphone from his belt holder. "I'll call my friend over in Malby's Crossing and see if he can examine you immediately."

"I thought you were a doctor." John finally got a word in.

"Plastic surgeon. He's an ob--"

"A female doctor. I'm having iron issues. Devon arranged an appointment. With one of his friends." Mary rushed the words out, too fast, and the sentences were short. She wasn't telling the truth. At least she wasn't telling all the facts. His little jewel was hiding something.

Her gaze clung to Devon as he walked into the kitchen talking into the phone. Phoenix wrapped her arm around Mary's waist and led her to the sofa.

"How about ordering pizza?" Phoenix suggested.

"Can't, it'll give me heartburn. I'll get a salad and you guys can have pizza. What if we order carry-out from Duck's place and have it delivered or pick it up?" Mary asked.

Devon held his thumb on top of the receiver. "Monday at eight AM. Okay for you?"

"Yes. Can you give me a lift?" Mary sat on the sofa and folded her legs under her.

Devon nodded and gave the affirmation into the cellphone. Obviously he'd come to care for Mary in the past three weeks. She had that kind of effect on people. Men and women, in a short period of time, came to love her. Her problem was, she trusted everyone.

"I'll take you to the doctor," John announced as he dragged a phone book from below the end table. What was going on? The three amigos were covering something.

"Devon will take me," Mary said, and directed a determined look at Phoenix.

She lifted an eyebrow. "I'm out of this little debate. Now that we've gone to the floral warehouse, I have to pack to go back to South Carolina."

Mary fell against the cushions and closed her eyes. "I don't want you to leave."

"I don't want to, but I must. I teach school, remember?" Phoenix kept her gaze on Devon. "I've a break in a few days and I'll return."

"You're not leaving my side, Mary, so get used to me hanging around." John flipped through the yellow pages, tearing a few as he did. "Write down what you want to order, and I'll call it in."

Phoenix scribbled on a slip of parchment. "Want a chef salad, Mary?"

As slow as a turtle, Mary went into her bedroom. Over her shoulder she said, "Yes. Sounds good, better than soft food."

Devon, having finished his phone call, sat across from John. Phoenix slid the list and pen into his hand and rushed into the bedroom.

"Write down what you want from Duck's." John glanced at the ladies to find them deep in conversation. "Waterman has been sighted in Vermont. I'm confident he's discovered that Mary's in Cage and he is determined to find her."

"Do you have a photo that we can post in our county sheriff's office and the surrounding counties to alert people?" Devon typed into his mobile.

"Yes. I've already sent his data to the local sheriff." John drew his briefcase from the sofa and sorted through the few documents he carried. "Average Joe."

"So ordinary features, height of..." Devon confirmed.

"Five seven. Here is a photo." Cellphone in hand, John brought Waterman's mug onto the screen.

"He could blend in anywhere. Brown hair, dark eyes, as you said, there's nothing outstanding about him." Devon rubbed his chin, the phone still snug in his hand. "We'll keep Mary within sight at all times. I'll call my office and try to rearrange some appointments for the next week."

"That won't be necessary. I'll always be at her side and protect her."

"You can investigate, while I protect her." Devon didn't meet his stare. He was withholding something, and John planned to find out what it was.

"I intend to keep her safe until the full truth about the case has been disclosed." John held out his hand for the carry-out list.

Devon wrote on the paper and slid it across the table top. "The way you look at Mary, I would have sworn you thought of her more than just a client needing a guard."

John tore the paper from his hand and stood. "That would be my private business."

The doctor firmed his lips into a straight line, but didn't get the chance to make a comment, as Phoenix came out of the bedroom.

"Dinner ready?" Phoenix asked.

"I'm going now." John nodded at Mary, who leaned against the bedroom door frame. "I'll be back in about thirty minutes. Stay inside."

"Okay. Thank you." She shot a look at him and then Devon. In the past few weeks, a relationship had developed between the two. Could it be stronger than a simple friendship? John hoped it wasn't intimate, because that would change now that he was back in her life. Christ, when had he become so alpha?

He climbed into his car and phoned in the food order. A quick call to his partner proved she was in a dead zone or her phone was out of service. John drove into the town of Cage. As he waited for time to pass before he could collect the food, he went to the two hotels in town. He flipped his phone to an image of Waterman and asked the clerk and any of the workers if they'd seen the man. All denied any knowledge of his whereabouts. Probably valid, as there were at least a hundred chalets in the vicinity for rent. Waterman could he hiding out in any one of those.

Tomorrow John would check out the bed and breakfasts.

Parking in front of Duck's, he shot from his BMW. Focused on Mary and the possibility she had a thing for the plastic surgeon, John held the door open for a guy walking out. His shoulder bumped into John's left arm. The lack of apology drew his attention. About his height, narrow face, full lips, long beard and languid-looking. The physical attributes nagged him.

"May I help you?" a tiny brunette asked. Her curls were held firm beneath a sailor's hat.

"Pick up for Kajiyama." Fuck! John fled the restaurant and glanced around the parking lot. He ran into the street, scoping the traffic, trying to see the man. It had to be Waterman. All of the characteristics, despite the full beard, fit the criminal.

Waterman was closer than John cared to imagine.

Chapter 18

"John, hand me the end of the ivy, please." Mary surveyed Mrs. Landware's transformed living room. The colonial furniture fit perfectly with the southern style Christmas trims. The elder woman was going to be very surprised.

"Didn't I tell you no climbing on ladders? That I would take care of everything requiring elevation?" She was sure his tone was meant to intimidate, so she stifled a laugh. He dipped to the floor, coming up with the fake vine dangling from his fingers.

She tucked the bit of ivy into the mass of pine boughs tacked near the crown molding. "Posh, I'm part monkey."

"Get down!"

Finished anyway, she held out her hand. As he reached for her, she fell directly into his arms. He "oomphed" and stepped back a few inches.

"I'm glad you're here, John." She kissed his cheek, inhaling his clove scented skin. His aftershave had a strong spice aroma. "I like your cologne."

"You're not going to distract me," he murmured, but touched his mouth to hers. Finally!

"I'm not trying to distract you." Her wrists rested on his shoulders. She trailed her tongue along the outline of his upper lip, capturing his mouth with hers and adding passion to the mix. An obvious connection existed between them, so why hadn't he shared her bed the past two nights?

His hunger was evident as he increased the pressure of their lips. He moved his hands to cup her hips and drew her steadily closer. Unable to resist, he broke the kiss and touched her earlobe. "No climbing at all and no going outside without me by your side. Got it? Also, you can't use the sheriff's deputies to decorate the yard with lights. They're here for surveillance only."

"Yeah, I know. We're lucky to have them, thanks to having made friends." Or Devon's influence, but she dared not mention his name or a scowl would form on John's face.

"Mary, I hardly recognized the living room. Oh, and the dining room is perfect, exactly as I wanted," Mrs. Landware said, entering. She fluttered her hands in front of her. "And it continues out onto the veranda. Oh, my."

John dropped his arms so fast, burns surely appeared on her skin. "Your house is beautiful, Mrs. Landware. I like the style. Colonial, right?"

The sweet lady's age-lined face brightened. Her smile had the same wattage as the recently installed string of lights. "Please call me Dorothy. Yes, the style is Colonial and I'm so pleased Mary is keeping the southern motif in the Christmas decorations."

Pine boughs, tiny candle-like lights, holly berries and bright red ribbon transformed the room. Traditional and in perfect keeping with the decor, Mary had added large fake magnolias and a twist of grape vines in the dining room. Fresh flowers and small pine trees were added throughout the large open house to bring in the fragrance of the season. White poinsettias against the cherry wood walls popped in glimmering sheen. Floral scents from the cut flowers, in addition to the pine, perfumed the air.

"Please, come into the receiving area, I want you to see the tree." Mary entwined Mrs. Landware's arm with hers.

"Hurry along young man, don't dally." Mrs. Landware urged John forward. A television broadcaster in the background indicated the ten o'clock news would be next. Made aware of the time, Mary's energy level plummeted. Devon had told her to expect tiredness with her pregnancy. She wanted to go home and rest.

A slight grin appeared on John's face. The guy was a trooper. They'd been decorating the massive house since eight that morning. Tomorrow, after she put the final touches on the gilded angel, she'd be finished.

Mrs. Landware stopped dead in her tiny tracks as they entered the foyer. "I need to sit down."

Gray seeped into her white face. John rushed forward and grabbed the dark green side Pulpit chair near the Scotch pine tree and placed the seat behind Mrs. Landware just as she dropped.

"Are you all right, Mrs. Landware, er, Dorothy?" Mary glanced at John.

He shrugged.

"Yes, dear." Maybe because of the death grip on her arm, the woman suddenly seemed frail. Tears hovered in her pain-filled eyes.

"I know we've stayed late. I'm sorry we kept you up." Mary loosened the gnarled hand, but caressed her shoulder.

"I'm a night owl," Mrs. Landware whispered, as if it were to remain a secret.

Mary knelt in front of her. "Then what has upset you?"

"Happy." She dug around in her pockets until she extracted a handkerchief. *Dorothy* had been embroidered in the corner, the red standing out on a bleached material. The finely woven cloth was misshapen with age. "Dear, you've made my dreams come true."

"The tree looks kind of plain to me," John said. He waved a hand toward the corner. "Just a few white lights and nuts."

"Not plain, but filled with folk art from my past. The corn husk pigs and flowers, the pine cone and..." Mrs. Landware coughed into her hankie, then rested her hands on the arms of the chair.

"Milk pod angels," Mary added, and stood. "I've been making the ornaments for the past two weeks."

"Felt clowns and birds. The peanuts all strung together to create a man. You used red ribbon for the hat and scarf--Yankee Doodle Peanut Man is what the decoration is called." She grabbed Mary's hand. "All of it is simply beautiful. You've brought my childhood forward. Thank you."

Mary had intended to use the handmade ornaments on her own tree, but the joy multiplied by sharing. "You know which one is my favorite?"

"The egg painted like a jewel?" John asked.

She narrowed her eyes. What was up with him consistently dropping hints about gems? His comments made anger seethe inside her. "No. My favorite is the teasel owl."

She released Mrs. Landware's hand and lifted a tiny wooden V from a vibrant green branch. "It has a tiny thistle nudged in the lower area of the oak tree stem. The eyes and nose are made from sunflower seeds, the red ribbon symbolizes love. The owl, wisdom. What more could you want than those two merged together to create a cute little Christmas adornment?"

"What more could you possibly want?" John's piercing brown-eyed stare was intense. She glanced away. Her heart flopped around behind her lungs. What underlying message was he trying to convey?

"What plans do you have for Thanksgiving?" Mrs. Landware dabbed at her eyes with the lacy corner of the hankie.

Mary lifted her gaze to John. Would she be in this city next Thursday? For that matter, would she be alive?

"Obviously, you don't have any plans except to eat at the Oink Cafe, so y'all come here and join my family and friends for Thanksgiving." Mrs. Landware let a smidgen of her southern past seep through her voice.

There weren't any guarantees at this stage in Mary's ever-intriguing life. She couldn't agree. The older woman reminded her so much of her own grandmother, with her immediate and sincere hospitality and southern gentry intonation. "Mrs. Landware--"

"I won't take no for an answer." Mrs. Landware energetically shot to a standing position, and waved at them as if to say *leave now and come back on Thanksgiving*.

* * * *

"We'd be delighted to join you and your family on Thanksgiving," John responded.

Dorothy, having regained her energy, shuffled to the front door. "Great, I'll see you then." She tugged the embellished silver handle opening the entrance. The jingle bells added music to the song coming from a commercial on the television.

John grabbed their coats from the gilt bench near the door.

"But I've--"

"Next week, Mary." Dorothy waved. "Night, John."

"Good night, Dorothy," John replied. On the veranda he assisted Mary in getting her jacket in place. Her body was stiff, and she didn't say anything. He was sure a tempest like Vermont had never experienced would come down in the form of Mary Keefe once they were en route to the guest house.

Twenty minutes later, the silence was more excruciating than a stern lecture from his father. John had to start the conversation, to say something positive. "I like your decorating style."

Her lips tightened, and she turned her face toward the passenger window.

"I expected something art deco, since your jewelry creation tends to be more deco-ish."

The least she could have done was comment on the word creation. Nothing. No response came from her pursed lips.

"Do you want to talk about whatever has gotten you into a tizzy?" He drove onto the primitive gravel road. The car wheels spun and loose stones pinged against the undercarriage. "You smell like cloves. How many little bags of the stuff did you put together last night?"

The doctor's car wasn't parked in front of the guest house. That, at least, was something to celebrate. The door lever clicked to open before he'd shut the motor down. Blasted little prima donna. Who did she think she was?

John was out of the car and inside the house, dutifully trailing her through the various excess from the job littering the living room. Pine boughs and holly berries sprinkled the small space, making it appear as if elves had scattered Christmas fucking cheer throughout the place.

He removed his overcoat and tossed it onto the coat rack, securing the cloth on a hook as if he were a pro basketball player. Pine branches blocked his path. He'd snapped them apart for her--and at midnight--and then he'd used a stinky Brillo-pad to get the sticky goo from his fingers. He glanced at his makeshift bed on the couch. The stem ends had seeped glue onto his blankets and a glob marked the top of his laptop. She had intentionally damaged his sleeping space. The spoiled brat.

He collected the limbs and picked up the remaining sticks. The fresh, woodsy scent didn't excite him as it had earlier. Anger grew. Why'd she place all of the stickiness on his bed? He glanced at her. She had to have known what she was doing. Her coat dropped. The parquet floor became the perfect resting place for the pungent gummy gunk. She stood beside her self-created work bench. The welding iron heated with its red dial blinking at him, as if to say *ha ha, you're the loser here.*

Having stood silent and still for the past few minutes, she finally met his stare. He shifted his gaze to her coat, to the branches, and then back to her face. Her eyes lit like fireworks in a summer sky. Obvious from her expression she was daring him. John grabbed the remaining handful of gooey twigs from the couch. He should get her attention, put the pine on her coat. He couldn't sleep on tacky sap. Crud she'd intentionally put on the sofa.

Mary rushed forward and grabbed his wrist. He held fast, not giving an inch.

Would she finally speak, ask forgiveness for her rude behavior?

She slid her pink tongue between her cupid lips, drawing his attention. His stomach clutched as she half-closed her eyes. Two steps drew him in position, his face aligned with hers. She'd apologize, and he'd zoom in with forgiveness and seal it with a kiss.

She snapped a few branches from his hand, and then slipped to the floor. He had to stop her. She was retrieving her Anorak. The fallen pine stems scattered into the foyer as she wrestled her jacket onto her side, tucking the slick material under her arm. John wrapped his branch laden arms around her waist. Unbalanced, they fell onto the floor, the puffy style coat softening the landing. Their tryst on the ship came fresh into his mind. His hand, which held the twigs, went over her head. His knee trapped her other arm, wrapped in the bright blue coat lining, snug to the hardwood.

"You excite me," he whispered into her ear. His voice, shallow and raspy, vibrated in his throat. And so unlike himself he wasn't sure what to think. She twisted his guts into knots.

"Then why do you sleep on the sofa instead of with me?" she responded in an equally soft, breathless tone.

"Oh, you didn't lose your voice after all."

"You infuriate me. You trot in here, holding a gun to my head, treat me like a criminal instead of a lover, so what am I to assume? That you were playing a role on board that ship and used me for a one-night hook-up while trying to get information? Did you care nothing for me? You claim a killer is trying to find me. What's your role now? My big-bad-protector? You constantly drop hints about the stolen diamonds." The words spewed from her mouth full throttle. She shoved his hand. A few twigs adhered to their skin. "Do you believe I was a part of the robbery, John?"

He couldn't respond. Each word she spoke drove a spike directly into his heart. Her viperous tongue sliced into his core. Had she never experienced real adoration? Maybe she didn't recognize true love when it kissed her face.

Her quick breaths pushed her breasts into his chest. John released his clutch on the pine boughs and she did as well. A toss, and the scented branches landed with the others on the foyer floor. Lifting his knee, he waited while she untangled herself from the coat. His fingers clasped hers, sticking them together like super glue, and then he moved their arms to the side stretched out, resembling the beautiful jeweled angel she'd created in the kitchen. He lowered his entire body to touch hers, while keeping the bulk of his weight off of her.

"Mary Keefe, I've never met anyone like you. The moment you crashed into my room, you stole my heart."

A striated hiss came from her, as if all of the pent-up steam had left her body.

He kissed her luscious red lips, a light brush. "I made love with you, but I wonder, are you really saying we banged, and anyone could have been in my place?"

Chapter 19

Bang Wang. Mary drew a sharp breath, feeling the wooden floorboards of the living room under her back. Scared of love, she wasn't going to admit anything, even if being in love with John had passed through her thoughts. As her friends had clearly pointed out, her choices for love interest in the past had been imperfect. She pressed her eyes closed. Mary Keefe was flawed.

He'd expect some sort of response. She needed to misdirect his attention. After all, she'd used the donor list, which would incriminate her. She licked her lips. "John, the night we were together I put aside all of my trepidations and goals, because I wanted to be with you. No banging, Wang or Kajiyama. The chaotic fears of the night disappeared when you touched me, and we moved in rhythm with the slow songs…your kisses."

The man was a fantastic kisser. If her fingers weren't coated with pine goo, she'd touch his mouth. Just to outline and commit the shape to memory. She wanted some implanted remembrance, in case. She wouldn't think of the future or the diamonds hidden on her purse.

"Yes? My kisses?" He touched his lips to hers. A supple nibble, and then he shifted, disconnecting their mouths.

The loss of his warmth was profound. Although she'd been shocked when Conrad robbed the store, her heart had quickly disconnected from him. She hadn't experienced a pang of remorse as she'd adamantly signed the police statement naming him as the thief. But John. Her separation from John and the possibility he sought her simply to prove her guilt, for a crime she didn't commit, hurt so much she couldn't breathe properly. She focused on his eyes. Soft, brown, sincere, the list could go on and on. She loved him and she'd break his heart when and if he found out the truth. "Your mouth does amazing things to mine. I can't get enough--"

He kissed her, the same fiery lip lock as when they'd made love. Yes, she admitted she had made love with him. Not as a result of a last minute grasp for impregnation. The bartender would have been able to provide a donation, but she'd wanted to be with John. The tempest he'd started in her during the wave ride had been eased that night.

Wanting to feel a connection again, she lifted her hips, pushing them against his. He nuzzled her neck. Her fingers remained stuck to his.

Beneath his nimble fingers, the pearl buttons of her sweater quickly come out of the holes and exposed her lacy white bra.

She didn't have as much luck with his Oxford, so she changed her strategy and licked the rich light brown skin at the V of his shirt, noting he'd kept his tan. He lifted his tantalizing mouth from her belly and nuzzled a breast. The material from the undergarment brushed against her skin, stimulating her. Excitement rushed through her, making her tingle in her nether region. Her nipple throbbed, while the other crested, waiting to be laved.

"My turn. Let me on top." His soft leather belt opened as she unhooked the buckle. Easy enough. His cock filled, pressed against his zipper, distracting her mouth from her goal of unlatching the silver bar from the hole on his belt.

Her efforts were futile. "Gun's in the way, biting into my side. I can't get the…need to touch."

The doorbell chimed. She whipped her glance toward the bothersome noise.

"Ignore it." His lips wet her nipples, striking her to the edge of manic desire.

Three raps sounded, followed by Dane's ear piercing shouts. "Mary. Mary, are you in there?"

"Dane won't go away. Let me get rid of him."

"No. I will." He slowly separated their hands. The sticky residue had congealed, stretching their skin during the separation. Her coat had no doubt been ruined by the pine sap.

She smiled. "Regret that action now?"

His hands landed on the floor beside her head, then he kissed her as hard and properly as the *thump, thump, thump* came from the wood door. "Not for a minute. I look forward to extending and finishing."

John catapulted to a stand with such grace and agility, she stared at him. He'd lost the love handles on his sides. Why hadn't she noticed before? Over the past few weeks his body had shaped into a well-muscled, sleek masculine form. He'd been beautiful before, but now he was diamond-head-gorgeous. All females would dig him. Her heart struck rapid beats against her ribcage. She didn't want other women to look at him, touch him, or be gifted with his exceptional kissing.

He held out his hand and helped her to stand. A nudge to her rear and she scooted forward into the bedroom. The click of a lock and a blast of cold air entered as she rushed into the bathroom. She ran hot water, trying to remove the pine scented glue.

He had to send Dane away. John had ignited a fire inside her, and she must get relief. The clack of a latch connecting caught her attention. She widened the door and glanced into the foyer mirror to see John's reflection. He didn't look happy. Crap. Sexual gratification would be delayed.

"What's wrong?" She strode toward him.

John wrapped his arms around her waist. His frown concerned her.

"Oh no, has something happened to Phoenix?"

"Not as far as I know. It's Waterman. He's close. He left something on Dane's car while it was parked at a Garden and Floral Design Center, with a warning for you. I need to take the note into the nearest station and try to get prints to qualify it as evidence."

She turned in his arms. "Okay, I'll stay here and work on the angel."

He kissed her cheek. "No. Sorry, but from this point on you'll need to stick to me." He held up his hands. "Like glue."

"As if I haven't been so far."

He drew back. "Seriously, Mary, I need to know where you're at every moment."

"What about work? I'm supposed to go back into the store since I've finished with Landware's project." She needed that job. It kept her busy, gave her a little cash and made her feel good about the chaos in her life. Recently she'd considered becoming a full-time floral designer. What if she could merge both, floral and jewelry? The angel! She could extend the post to the figurine and make it part of a flower arrangement.

"I'll talk to the owner."

Pivoting, she walked into the living room. "I like my job, and I've bills to pay. If Frank finds out I'm the target of a nut case then he might not keep me."

"Frank?"

"Frank Cartwright. He owns the Garden and Floral Design Center about a mile away. I work part-time for him." She lifted her hair, knotting it at the nape of her neck. "He'll be afraid I'll attract a shooter and his business will be destroyed. Damn, what a mistake."

"Ah, that explains why you decorated the house and made the craft ornaments."

"Show me what Waterman actually looks like, and if he comes close, I'll run. I've a cellphone again, so I could call."

He took both of her arms in his hands. "You must not understand how much he wants to get to you. This man got out of jail the day before he robbed the jewelry store, after serving a sentence for assaulting his lifelong friend. Waterman will kill you without taking a second breath."

"What if we gave him the diamonds?" she whispered.

He stepped back and palmed the gun snug in the leather holster at his side. "What?"

"Don't get all militant on me. I found them the first night of the cruise. I was unpacking my shoes, the stretcher came out and the diamonds were in the pointed toe. After I left you at the elevator, I spent the night shoving agates out of the prongs, putting the diamonds in and sewing a casing over them to make sure I didn't lose one." She bit her lip. Had she just ended what she hoped would be the beginning of a great relationship?

"You didn't tell the police because…"

"Knock that suspicious frown off your face. I wanted to give them directly to my grandfather, to prove to him I could be responsible. Because Conrad attacked me, I couldn't. I've been in survival mode."

"Mary," he said, his voice resembling a bear's growl. "You could have gotten that message across by turning them into the captain, or first mate, before you were attacked."

"Okay, now you're really intimidating me."

His arms relaxed. He took her hand into his sticky one and led her to the sofa, avoiding the cloth coated with pine sap. "Tell me the rest."

Not sitting down, she licked her lips. She freed her hand and tucked both under her armpits as cold invaded her. Confrontations weren't her thing. "I was afraid I'd be arrested and my time on the ship would end. I considered giving them to the police once we docked. Would you have left them in the shoes? No, of course not. Don't forget, I was on the ship to de-stress, and well, you know why people go on cruise." Her voice sharpened. "Maybe you don't, since you were there to follow me?"

"Where are the diamonds?" he snapped.

"In the bedroom." She strode into the room, which a few minutes ago she had hoped would be her place of pleasure. "Could you get that suitcase on the top shelf of the closet?"

John snagged the beaten brown leather satchel and placed it on the bed. He threw a few articles of black clothing out, then tipped it over. "Does it have a false bottom?"

She picked up the white evening bag and held it out. "Here they are."

He took the purse and tilted it in the light. "Very clever."

"Uncut stones generally don't give off a lot of sheen, so only a few striations sparkle. Each one is kind of in a claw, but to make sure it was safe I sewed a second trap to keep them snug. Now you know why I was exhausted that day at the wave pool."

His smile at the mention of the pool quickly became a frown. "You carried this purse to dinner."

"Yes, and no one suspected it was decorated with a million dollars' worth of gems." She shoved hair behind her ears.

"I've lost my edge." He stared at her neck. "You could have been killed."

"But I wasn't. I wanted to keep the diamonds close in case I needed leverage. My life for stolen jewels. Wouldn't the cops forgive me for the exchange?" Suddenly exhausted, she plopped onto the bed.

Determination etched his face. "There isn't forgiveness with the law. White or black, follow the rules or break them, but there isn't a gray area." His firm voice sent skitters along her arms.

"So, are you going to turn me in?"

Chapter 20

John gazed at Mary sprawled on the bed seemingly relaxed. But her right eye twitched. He'd noticed the eye jerk a couple of times when she got angry. Too strong a word--rather, when she got annoyed. "Do you want me to say yes so you can ignore the fact we're right for each other?"

He carefully laid the diamond embossed bag on the colorful quilt and walked around the bed. Straddling her legs to keep her from running away, again, he said, "Look at me."

A fine coat of unshed tears held steady in the corners of her eyes.

"Why are you afraid to love?" he whispered.

She snorted, a funny little rough gurgle. "Trust me when I tell you I'm not afraid to love. On the contrary, I love too easily and have made very bad choices in the past. My heart is closed for renewal."

"I warn you, Mary Keefe, I plan to open your heart." He brushed a kiss on each side of her eyes and then her mouth. "Go get ready. We're going to South Carolina."

She bolted upright. "I work tomorrow. Busy time of the year, with Thanksgiving next week. Why can't I stay here and go with Devon to his house?"

John grabbed the purse and removed his cellphone from his pocket. "Because I'm not letting you out of my sight." He lifted his fingers. "We're stuck like glue."

She went into the bathroom and John made his way to the kitchen. After putting the bag and his phone on the bar, he ran water to a close boiling point and scrubbed his hands, getting the pine sap off. As he dried his fingers, he glanced at the boughs littering the living area. So much for romancing her. At least she'd admitted to having the jewels. If only he could get her to confess the other secret she kept hidden. She wasn't good at keeping her feelings buried. He doubted she could tell a lie. He'd find out what Mary was hiding, so they could begin their relationship with a clean slate.

He opened the cabinets until he found a blue cloth sack with a pair of shoes imprinted on the outside. The purse would fit perfectly. Shoving the handbag inside the bag, he placed it on the counter, and then picked up his cell.

A quick punch to speed dial number thirty-three, double D. "Debbie. Where are you?"

"Pulling in beside your car. What's up with the gravel driveway? It's messing the paint on my Mercedes."

"Bring your luggage. I've got a job for you."

"My messenger bag is not luggage. Jack Georges makes the very best protected environment. John, are you all right?"

He blew out a harsh breath. Mary had come from the bedroom dressed in a snug crimson sweater, which gave her a pretty blush and brought out red tints in her hair. She smiled. Her painted-on jeans exemplified every curve of her luscious body.

"Yeah. I'll open the door so you can shove the fifty pounds inside." He snapped his phone shut, cleared his throat and focused on his woman. "Ready?"

Two raps, a pause and two taps--Debbie's secret knock resounded through the room.

Mary glanced at the entrance and then at him. "Expecting company?"

"Just my partner." He brushed past her. "Excuse me."

John threw the locks and slowly opened the entry. Debbie barreled through, tossing the dead weight of a briefcase onto his chest. Off balance, he fell against the wall, and the luggage dropped to the floor with a thud. She stepped over the case and pressed her body tight to his.

"Hello, lover." She kissed him. Full on the mouth, with her knee painfully pressed between his legs, smashing his cock.

He broke the kiss and pressed her shoulders, forcing her body away from his. What game was she playing?

"Miss me?" She zoomed in for another lip lock.

Mary cleared her throat, twice. "Do you want me to leave?" she asked, her frosty tone biting more than the nor'easter cold front due to arrive that night.

"Enough, Debbie." The words came out loud enough Bushard could have heard him in the big house.

Debbie stuck her cheek to his shoulder. "Hi, I'm Debbie. I think we met on the cruise ship."

"Yes, I remember," Mary shot back.

With his knee, he dislodged Debbie's leg from its uncomfortable location. He slid from behind her and waved between the two. "Mary, Debbie Gilbert is my partner. We are not involved. We're co-workers, at least until this case is over."

"So you all just change your last names to track down insurance fraud?" Mary asked.

Debbie didn't appear to have heard. She clung to the back of his shirt as if it were a life preserver.

"This is the situation." John twisted from her clutches and strode toward the kitchen. He grabbed Mary's hand and snagged the blue bag. Purse tucked under his arm, he jerked the blankets, scattering twigs and bits of brush everywhere in the living room.

Debbie righted her luggage and dragged it to the couch. She plopped on the edge of the sofa closest to where he stood. "Out with it."

He sat, pulling Mary onto the sofa snug against him. Extracting the purse, he held it out. "The diamonds are attached. I need you to take it to Florida and turn in the jewels, then have them replaced with imitations. I also have a threatening note found on Bushard's car to be logged in at the local police station."

Mary demurely folded her hands on her lap.

Debbie took the handbag, catching the afternoon light in the exposed facets. The illuminations made prisms on the ceiling and walls. She caught his stare, and shifted her gaze to Mary. "She was involved after all. I told you not to trust the quiet ones."

Mary harumphed. "Who do you--"

"She wasn't part of the robbery." He looked at Debbie's red hair, about the same texture and length of Mary's. Her body structure was very similar. "I want to set up a sting. Could you get a wig or color your hair to match Mary's?"

Debbie's smile widened. "Yes. This is what an investigative agent is supposed to do. We've never tried to apprehend the criminals, just write reports. This is going to be awesome."

"She's going to pretend to be me?" Mary scraped hair away from her face. "Can she design?"

Debbie stared at him, her eyes bright with anitcipation.

"Mary's working as a floral designer. With the help of the local law, we can trap Waterman," John announced.

Debbie rubbed her hands together. "Great. Stash the singlet and let's get crazy."

Mary jumped from the sofa and marched into the bedroom. The wooden door crashed against the jamb.

John slowly rose. "You can sleep on the couch."

Debbie laughed. "Trouble in paradise?"

Pausing at the exit, he turned. "Waterman is psycho-dangerous. The note was attached to a mutilated rabbit. Don't leave her alone and don't say anything to her."

"You mean about you and me bumping and grinding?" she said a little louder than normal.

With narrowed eyes, he glared at her. "We never did anything of the sort. What's up with you?"

Debbie meandered around the coffee table and ran her pointed, purple enameled fingernails down his chest. "We're partners and belong together. She's not the one for you."

He jerked away, grabbed his coat and glanced at her. "Your next partner will be the lucky one. You'll guide him through the steps. I'm going to reassure Bushard. I'll return in a few minutes."

* * * *

The bedroom door's hinges vibrated, squeaking in rebellion of being slammed. Mary plopped onto the soft cushion of the overstuffed blue, yellow and white checked chair. Would she never learn? She'd fallen in love with a man who might not be into commitment. If she were reincarnated, she'd hope to be a Mallard duck or a wolf. They selected a mate and remained true to each other until death did they part. Her friends were right; she always made bad choices in love.

Tomorrow she was supposed to get the stitches removed, if she remained in Cage. Devon. He felt sympathy for her. He'd take her to her doctor's appointment and help her to escape this deplorable situation. John had the diamonds, and clearly that's why he'd been searching. She touched her stomach. Her baby needed her to make the right choice, and by staying too, Dane, Frank and Tim would be in jeopardy. Selfishness and uncontrollable fear had to be subdued. Being single didn't make her an invalid needing assistance from a man. She'd stand alone and play John's investigation game sensibly. No, she wanted her baby to be safe. She had to leave Cage.

Mary dug the pill bottles out of the bedside drawer and went into the bathroom. After brushing her teeth, she ran water in a glass and downed the doses. A flick of the shower's knob and water cascaded. She stripped, stepped into the tub, pulled the curtain and simply enjoyed the magic of warm liquid sliding over her. Moments later she exited, dried herself and dressed in a loose tee and tap-pant underwear. After sliding a comb through her hair, she crawled beneath the covers. The night John arrived, Devon had just whispered congratulations, that she was indeed pregnant. When would she start to show? She hoped she wouldn't simply pop out. It would be difficult to explain the expansion, since her appetite was non-existent. Of course, a rounded belly would be nice to see, a sign of her baby. Some indication to prove the bit of new life was alive and well. Miscarriage was still a possibility.

What would the next day hold for her? Was John in the living room banging Debbie, his more-than-work partner? No, he wasn't that kind of guy. Despite everything that had happened, she knew he was good and honest.

The television came on, loud, an MTV or similar type station filling the space with hot, fast music. Good, the background noise would cover whatever was going down. Mary tried to block out the murmurings, but her heart wouldn't let her. Shifting onto her side, she slid her head between the pillows. Muted thumps from the bass, and squealing she hoped came from the singer, made their way through the cotton and feathers. She hummed a church hymn, which quickly turned into *Rescue Me* by Aretha Franklin, "Oh, take me in your arms and rescue me, da da da." She couldn't remember the words, so she hummed the tune.

Crap, what was the rest of the line? "I'm blue and I need you."

A weight lowered beside her. John, singing in a seductive voice, "Come on and rescue me. 'Cause I need you, by my side. Can't you see that I'm lonely. Rescue me."

Mary opened her eyes. Lips slightly parted, she joined him in the next part. "Come on and take my heart."

John placed his hands on the pillows, lowering them beside her head. He held her gaze. "Together, we can make powerful music."

His hands felt cold, as if he'd just come in from outside. He caressed the side of her cheek and lifted a wet sliver of hair. Her breathing picked up speed, and her stomach muscles contracted. As he lowered the strand, he caressed her clavicle and the soft, dark skin of his wrist connected with the crest of her ivory breast. Their little tryst in the living room rushed into her thoughts. Her nipples peaked.

"Are you going to ask me to sleep in the chair, or do you think you might have room in this cozy bed?" He stroked her arm and held steady at her hand.

"What about sex on a red stick?" She nodded toward the living room. The door was shut, but the music continued to shake the rafters.

Had a chuckle caught in his throat? "Debbie and I work together. Period. No personal ties. The only woman I've slept with or wanted to be with in the last three months has been you."

"What about your hot kiss with her on the cruise ship?" The snarky comment popped out before she could control it.

"I only wanted to make you jealous. The moment you crashed into my room, you stole my jewel," he whispered.

A bump to his thigh and she scooted to the edge. "You can share my space."

"Thanks. I'll just shower off the rest of the pine sap." He pressed their fingers together to illustrate or remind her, they would be stuck like glue.

A dark substance coated some of the digits. His touch, so soft, hadn't stuck them to her face. Her heart sang in a fast happy cadence. They'd be together. If she got lucky, they'd finish what they'd started earlier. Mary licked her lips. "Okay."

His grin widened into a smile. An unsatisfying light kiss, and he catapulted from the mattress. "Keep the bed warm."

Chapter 21

John rushed through the shower, hoping to catch Mary all soft and dewy, in that want-to-have-sex position he'd left her. If not for the stickiness on his arms, he'd have skipped the shower and made love with her immediately. But he couldn't. She deserved some respect and he'd show her such. A couple of squirts of coconut-lime soap on a scratchy sponge and he gouged his skin with the rough edges, hurrying to get the sap removed.

Wrapping a towel around his waist, he ran a comb through his hair, and left the steamy bathroom. Mary's pink top and panties were piled on the floor. If he had any karma at all, she'd be naked under the light sheet that barely shielded her lush breasts.

"Get the pine sap off?"

Like a green boy, he couldn't speak, so he nodded. The wet towel fell to the floor with a soft whoosh.

Eyes wide but full of caution, she tossed the covers to the side.

"Tell me I'm not dreaming." His cock, painfully engorged, jutted toward her.

"If so, we're together. I hope to make the fantasies I've had about you over the past three weeks come true. Obviously, you're up for the challenge." The wariness disappeared and her smile went full throttle.

He trailed his fingers along her wrist. Moving closer, Mary shoved John onto his back and climbed on top. Their chests touched and thighs rubbed against each other. He found his way to her sweet place with his cock, stroking her clit with the tip as he caressed one of her nipples with a thumb and forefinger.

Her lips worked magic as she nibbled on the side of his neck, then outlined his mouth with hers and sucked, until she inserted her limber tongue inside. He added hot passion. She moaned, making him want more, to taste more, experience more. She broke the kiss, placed a hand on his chest.

"So strong," she whispered and licked his nipple. The scents of coconut and lime filtered into his nostrils as his skin heated.

He rolled on top of her, parted her thighs and settled into place, the tip of his sensitive cock seeking to enter. But she wasn't ready. She didn't wiggle underneath him, squirm with excitement for him to fill her. No moaning, or groans because he wasn't inside her yet. Although they'd only been together one time, he knew exactly what to expect, what moves to make and when to merge their bodies.

God, she tasted good, hot and sweet, and the eager way she kissed him back sent shivers of delight through him. He wanted her so badly, her liquid heat surrounding him, and soon. His penis nodded as if in agreement of what was to come. She was wet, slick with desire when he inserted two fingers into the path he'd take to bring her to ecstasy. Her hips met his every stroke, and he moved his lips to her nipples, laving, sucking. She groaned, gripped his rear and tugged him closer.

"Now," she whispered.

He released a nipple and kissed her mouth, which she opened, welcoming him, and he entered her. Soon, they got into the rhythm of their own particular timing. The slap of their thighs kept beat with the thunk of drums on the current song playing in the other room. A tune he wasn't familiar with, but the *rata-tat-tat* was in perfect harmony.

He'd fantasized for such a long time about their second lovemaking session, he was ready to come within seconds, but he waited. She should have her pleasure before he took his. He withdrew, holding the end of his cock still inside her, and rubbed the tip of her clit with his fingers. Her pupils dilated, and she lifted her hips, driving herself deep. Her sleek, wet muscles surrounding his cock tightened, her moans became short bursts of air as her climax gathered.

A sharp moan came from her as she reached her summit. At her cry of pleasure, he couldn't help it and lost himself in her, filling her. His arms wobbled with the stress of holding most of his weight from pressing her into the mattress. Wanting to maintain the connection, he rolled to his side, keeping them attached.

"You're amazing," she whispered into his shoulder. Her warm breath dried the light coating of sweat on his skin.

He withdrew and positioned their bodies to align, listening to the music, and touching his lover. Something he hadn't been a part of for a long time.

Silence invaded as the stereo shut off. Mary had to leave Cage. He couldn't put her in danger, and menace was around the corner. He held her hand, and then kissed her cheek. "Until Waterman is caught, you're going to relocate to a safe house."

"No. I want to stay. I won't go out. I'll keep making crafts."

"Mary." He gripped her arm. "I'm not going to take chances with your life."

She pried his fingers loose, but held tight to his hand. "What about Mrs. Landware and Thanksgiving next week? The fake Mary will not get past her eagle eyes. The entire town will know."

"I'll cancel."

"She's old and values each encounter with people. You witnessed her expression just from viewing the tree. She longs for the good ole days when life was simple, and you could count on your neighbor helping in an emergency, or just being a friend and visiting. She'd probably be offended if we didn't show up. I know I've only lived in Cage for a short time, but I like the people and they like me. They would want to help. What if we left directly after Thanksgiving?" Her sea green eyes pleaded with him.

"This isn't up for negotiation. Debbie will imitate you, and you'll go to a safe house."

"I could stay at Devon's lake cottage, an hour away. As I've proven, sometimes it's best to hide something valuable in plain sight." She licked her lips.

He hated it when she did that, because her mouth was delectable and always drew his attention, especially when she made her lips slick and shiny. "Yes. You are valuable, which is the reason I'm not taking chances."

"I'll stay inside the entire time." She sat upright, drawing the sheet with her, and tucked it under her armpits. "Hire a guard. Keep the blinds closed. Hopefully, you'll catch Waterman and then we'll go to Mrs. Landware's dinner party. Let me be a decoy for Waterman. We'll be sure to draw him into the open."

"This isn't some TV show where they always catch the bad guys." He tugged the sheet and settled his back against the iron headboard. "I can get you a house in a warmer climate."

"My blood is beginning to get thicker. I don't want to run. I'd rather stay and fight."

"Fighting might include death, a risk I'm not willing to take." He glanced at her wound, which wasn't red and swollen. He had to admit Buckley had done an exceptional suturing job. "Let me sleep on it."

"Fine. We'll talk tomorrow." She gave a half-smile, turned onto her side, and placed her hands under the pillow.

Wanting their connection to last, he curved himself around her. She couldn't remain in the area. He'd have to be cautious in telling her no, because their relationship was new and fragile. A fiery blast would occur when he did, but he wasn't gambling with her life.

* * * *

The annoying constant buzz of the alarm woke her. Mary felt around until she found the off button. Eight o' clock. She had one hour until she had to be at work at the Garden and Floral Design Center. Today she planned to create an angel vignette. The wire figure would rest on a bed of baby's breath and white larkspur, to dangle in the display window.

Her usual roll to her back met resistance. Firm muscles, skin smelling of her body wash and sex. John.

"Good morning." He kissed her cheek and then catapulted off the bed.

As he strutted around the bed, heading toward the bathroom, she appreciated his tight rear. "I smell coffee. Have you been up already?"

"No. Debbie. She made a run to the bakery for breakfast. She's an early riser." He shut the door and then the water ran.

"Oh, Debbie," Mary murmured, knowing he couldn't hear her. Had John decided if she could stay? If the answer was no, then she would insist on going to the OB-GYN before he shipped her off. She needed to be told that her baby was safe and healthy. Once she got affirmation, she'd tell John fatherhood was in his future. She had no expectations from him, but being the daddy of their child and currently intimate with her, he should be told. Would he accept the news with joy? Was it a possibility that he'd connect the donor project with her pregnancy? She hadn't planned on him being a sperm benefactor, and after seeing Conrad on the ship, she'd abandoned the idea of conception. Her time with John was a result of desire and love. He had not been a target on a list of possible benefactors.

Mary rose, slipped on her robe and smoothed her hair. The bedroom door squeaked as she pulled it open, making her a little annoyed. She didn't want to surprise the unexpected houseguest who'd invaded her home.

Situated on the sofa, Debbie typed rapid fire on the keypad of a laptop. From the way she was positioned, her skin-tight white shirt rode high on her waist and thong underpants were visible. The woman irritated her. John could have been the first one out of the bedroom. Why wouldn't she be fully dressed if she'd gone to the bakery? Debbie gave a weak smile, sat upright and lifted her take-out coffee container. "Where's Kajiyama?"

"In the shower." She had to get rid of the actress. The longer Ms. Debbie squatted in the guest house the more time the woman would have with John. The chick wanted to be a fake Mary Keefe. More than likely she'd want all the benefits that came along with the name. But John's kisses and lovemaking would only be directed toward the real Mary.

The pungent aroma of coffee filtered into the air as Debbie lowered her cup. Mary made her way to the kitchen, intending to start a pot of tea. There were two other cups in the cardboard container on the bar. One Styrofoam cup had *caffeine free Chai* printed across the side. Perfect. Why not drink the fresh cup right in front of her?

She removed the plastic cap and poured the steaming creamy liquid into a ceramic cup.

"There are bagels and doughnuts," Debbie proclaimed in her nasally tones.

Mary flicked a finger and the white wax-coated bag popped open. She took hold of a shiny-crusted bagel. The fresh cinnamon aroma took her back to a simpler time, in her South Carolina kitchen, before Conrad had appeared in her life. She opened the fridge and glanced through the limited food products inside. Between the half-gallon of one percent milk and a loaf of bread was a box of cream cheese. Phoenix had gone shopping before she left.

Mary cut the bagel, tossed the two halves in the toaster and then retrieved the knife, wove the blade and turned it over between her fingers. Dexterity was a part of her genetics, because her mother had been a member of a knife throwing act with a traveling circus. The Cutting Edge troupe had left the city of Keefe with one less knife flicker, and her father had gained a wife. The knife was sharp, and she might need a weapon. She wiped it on the towel and slid it into her purse on the stool.

"Good morning," John said, his voice cutting across the room.

Mary was getting used to his light steps and knew the moment he came close.

She hadn't anticipated his arms circling her waist, nor his warm lips kissing her neck on the opposite side of the incision. "Um, smells good."

"Shall I warm one for you?" She turned into him, and found the sensitive part of his earlobe with her mouth. In the background, Debbie lowered her gaze and moved the laptop onto her naked thighs.

"Yes, please, I'm starving."

"I found a house for Mary," Debbie shouted from the living room.

Mary grimaced. The toaster shot the bagel up. Jerking the slices from the appliance, she placed them on plates, smeared cream cheese on top and handed one to John. He snapped his coffee from the counter, and with smooth even steps, went into the adjoining room. He took a seat on a foot stool and placed his dishes on the table. "Where?"

"California wine country. In the West she'll be hidden safely among the vines. Jason Fox will be her guard." Debbie typed a few key strokes. "Come see."

John sat beside his co-worker and evaluated the screen. Would he agree, or consider Mary's request? "Nice. I don't want Fox, though."

"Ho. Ho. Cause he's like a fine glass of wine, sensually handsome with a touch of age?" Bombshell's lips puckered.

The two investigators discussed her future as if she wasn't there. Mary finished the bagel, wiped her hands on a towel and snapped open a canvas shopping bag lying on the counter. She unscrewed the vise, laid it to the side and lowered the asbestos pads into the bottom of the carrier. The chunky vise went next. She grabbed a few plastic shopping sacks from under the sink, wrapped the angel in them and placed it on top. Her emergency escape satchel had been packed with what was important, her jewelry tools. Next stop was wine country, where she'd be protected by a George Clooney look-a-like.

Granted, neither the guard's appearance nor George's name had been mentioned, but if she was going to California and would be under house arrest, at least she could create whatever fantasy she wanted, including celebrating not going to jail for conspiracy or obstructing justice. The phone rang as she cleaned crumbs from the counter top. Mary ignored it, believing the ring tone belonged to John's cell.

"Mary," John said. He extended her open cellphone to her. "It's Devon."

She looked at John, at the phone and then at Debbie, who obviously planned to continue listening. Mary took the cell. "Hi, Devon, what's up?"

"My friend is going out of town but is willing to see you today. Can you get away to see the great Dr. Lance Secreast, OB-GYN?"

"When?"

"In one hour. If you leave in the next half-hour, you'll make it to his office in the village near Hillside on time."

John leaned against the counter with one dark eyebrow raised.

Mary kept her gaze on him. "Yes. Tell him I'll be there. Will you send me the address?"

"Yes, I'll text the details." Devon hesitated. "Do you need me to drive you? I'm at a hospital with a couple of emergency patients, but I'll get someone else to take them if you want."

"No, I'll be fine. If needed, I'll borrow Dane's car. Thank you for the offer."

Papers shifted in the background, and then Devon asked, "Okay if he removes your stitches?"

"I don't know. Once you've had magical fingers touch you, it's difficult to think of another's hands."

Arms crossed, John shot away from his lazy position.

Devon chuckled. "You can decide after you talk to Lance. He's a great guy, but if you want me to do the honors, then we can meet later tonight or tomorrow."

Tonight or tomorrow, she wouldn't be in Cage, Vermont. "Sure, I'll call you. Thank you for arranging the doctor's visit for today. I'll leave in the next few minutes."

Disconnecting from the call, Mary quickly dialed the Garden Center and talked to Betty, who snorted as Mary explained she was ill and would be out for the next two days.

Now, how to break the news.

Chapter 22

The sporting and business magazines in the lobby of the obstetrician slash gynecology office were limited. Many of them had teeth marks on the edges. John grabbed a gardening periodical off the glass tabletop and flipped through the pages, getting an idea of what was inside. The last selection of reading material would be parenting journals. He hadn't thought about children, since he'd never considered a permanent relationship, at least not until recently.

The woman sitting across from him was dressed in a fashionable business outfit, white blouse, vest and matching slacks. She used her PDA, sharp purple-painted nails clicking. He could envision Mary pregnant with his child. Not that she would wear an outfit like that, but one of the other more feminine selections he'd seen in the chick-oriented business magazines he'd flipped through. Instead of focusing on technology, Mary would smile in that sweet relaxed way she had, while touching her protruding stomach. Her eyes would be soft and dewy with love and hope. John shook off the image and reached for another decorating-how-to publication.

The slam of a file drawer brought his attention to the reception desk. A tiny nurse wearing pink scrubs and a stethoscope necklace reached for a file folder. The sharp-tongued dark-haired woman, who barked at Mary for not having an appointment or having filled out the documents prior to arriving, extended a manila envelope. Her sour expression must be permanent.

"Did she get impregnated by a sperm donor, or do you think hunky Dr. Buckley is the father?" the dark haired woman asked the nurse. "He arranged the visit and said it had to be hush-hush." Her attitude was as black as her hair.

"Obviously you don't know the meaning of hush. It's really none of our business. Just give me the pregnancy care instructions," the spunky nurse replied.

The landline rang, interrupting whatever unkind comment Miss Personality had on the tip of her wicked tongue. Around him, those in the waiting room flipped magazine pages. The nurse at reception shuffled papers and answered the phone.

His heart pounded in his chest as fast as the woman's typing on her tiny keyboard. Donor. Mary's list on the ship was labeled *donor*. Her categories weren't a sort of schematic for a potential dating partner, rather, a method to search for a perfect father, or at least the right sperm. Mary was pregnant. She'd failed to mention that little tidbit during her confession time.

He clenched his fists and the magazine ripped at the bottom. He wasn't on her donor list. Yet, she'd slept with him and he hadn't used protection. The coffee in his stomach churned. Had she been pregnant at the time? Who was the investor for Mary Keefe's child?

"John? Mr. Kajiyama?" Mary stumbled over his last name, as if having difficulty saying the word.

"Yes," he croaked.

"Ready to go, or would you like to finish reading that article?" Papers stuck out from her large purse. Eyebrows lifted, she stared at him. His hesitation was obvious, so he'd need to cover until they were alone.

He placed the nearly shredded magazine on the chrome and glass table and stood. "Yes, I'm ready. Everything okay?"

"Iron poor blood, as I expected. Could we stop by a pharmacy?" She didn't look him directly in the face, rather shifted her glance from the people in the waiting room to the receptionist, who hovered as close as possible to where they were standing.

"I'm sure there's nothing to worry about." He kept his voice at a monotone, while rage heated his insides. She was deceitful. No, the problem wasn't lies. It was that she didn't trust him. Heart pounding and gut painfully clenching, he took her elbow and led her toward the exit.

"Good bye, Ms. Keefe, will Dr. Buckley be coming with you next time?" the receptionist shouted across the room.

Mary tensed under his fingers. "Not that I know of, but I'll give him your regards, Michelle."

The glass doors gave him a ready view to the outside. Nothing unusual, so he relaxed. He should give Mary the benefit of doubt, or he was an idiot and had been used to be her baby's daddy. He took her hand and guided her to the car. Once she was strapped in the seat, he settled behind the steering wheel. She dug a gold tube out of her purse, twisted the bottom until pink appeared and refreshed her bow-shaped lips.

How in hell was he going to introduce the topic of the baby? He had to know, be able to confirm or shrug aside the gossip in the doctor's office.

The hum of the motor added a cadence to his thoughts as he rehearsed what he wanted to say and intended to ask. He shifted into *drive*. In front of them, a navy minivan raced out of the parking lot, disregarding speed limits.

John slowly pulled into the center of the lane and merged with the heavy traffic. He didn't mind the slow progress--it gave him time to sort information. Mary's focus remained on the window. Two stops later, he'd decided how to approach the donor topic and glanced at her. "Mary, I want to ask--"

She pointed with her index finger to the right. "Look, there's Bailey's Pharmacy, exactly where the nurse said it would be."

He drove into the parking lot. The blue van, visible in his rearview mirror, turned as well. The driver was a woman, shoulder length white hair, large red lips and enormous gold hoop earrings. How had she gotten behind them? Seatbelt snapped free from the latch, he released his cellphone. He absolutely hated field work.

"Why don't you stay here? You can see me enter and exit. I'll run in, get the scrip filled and be right out."

Torn between needing to protect her and getting the license plate number of the vehicle, he surveyed the lot. Half-filled. He'd parked near the pharmacy's glass entrance. "Fine, in and out. Do you have the cell?"

"Yes." She sighed as if the question was ridiculous.

Mary hurried into the pharmacy. A few minutes later a narrow-faced bleached blonde reached her bony fingers to tug her red dress free from clinging to her black overcoat, and walked past him.

He waited until she crossed over the threshold of the entrance. Extracting his keys, he got outside the car and glanced at the van's green license plate. The sun hadn't burnt off the fog, and the gold star on the tin stood out like a beacon in the grayness. Mary stood at the check-out.

John dialed Debbie.

"I'm driving through hell, what do you want?" Debbie answered.

"Ah, at the turnpike are you?" Debbie hated driving in heavy traffic. He ran toward the entrance of the pharmacy. His gut twisted into knots. Something wasn't right.

"Damn. Move!" Debbie snarled.

Mary closed her handbag, grabbed the paper sack, and the electric double doors opened. "Debbie, I need you to check out two things, Lance Secreast, gynecologist, and Vermont license plate number three-oh-oh-seven."

"Hum, the plot thickens. What does he have to do with the case?"

"Not sure. The license plate is on a navy blue minivan, Honda Odyssey. I urgently need the data on the van as a female, Caucasian, forties, is following us." John looked past Mary and into the store. Where was the blonde?

"Right. Stay out of trouble, Kajiyama." *Click clack* and the call ended. He stowed the phone on his belt holder.

John met Mary and wrapped his arm around her waist. They walked to his black BMW. Her muscles tensed under his hand, but he ignored the change and tugged the handle on the passenger side. Her seatbelt on, he shut her door and then climbed behind the driver's wheel. He glanced at her. "Want some lunch?"

"Devon mentioned a diner at the edge of town called Last Chance. What do you think about trying authentic local cuisine?"

"Fantastic." His focus remained on the pharmacy.

"Is everything okay?"

"Umm-hum, just cautious." He started the engine.

* * * *

The impending snow had created a gray pall on the day. Not even the quaint ranch-style restaurant cheered him. No neon signs for Last Chance. A simple wooden shingle swung on chains a few feet from the short staircase leading to the wrap-around porch. A light freezing wind blew the sign, making the links squeak as it moved to and fro in the breeze. Fresh fallen snow had created a frosting on the roof and banister of the porch. Fortunately, the sidewalks had been shoveled. Smokers puffed on cigarettes or cigars as they rocked in chairs, keeping to the right of the door. How could they tolerate the frigid whisks of air?

"The building is adorable. What do you think? Want to try *original Vermont fare*?" Mary had taken the words from the billboard. Her seatbelt zipped into its holder.

"Let's get carry out."

"I'm starving and I need to see people," she whined.

"Eat and leave. You stay with me the entire time." Releasing the fastener of his safety belt, he glanced in the mirrors. His gut instinct told him to avoid the place.

She stared at him as if he were an alien. "All right."

He flew around the car, threw open her door and clasped her hand in his. He held onto her, not wanting to lose any connection. A quick trip up the stairs and they were inside, smelling a bit of heaven as the aroma of pancakes with sweet maple syrup mingled with roasted meat.

He inhaled. "I can't decide which scent I like best."

"Umm, I know." Mary bit her perfect-shaped lip.

A public notice was posted at the end of the short hall. *"Find a seat wherever you can, and I'll be right with you.* That must be a motto in Vermont." John glanced through the area, noting each diner within sight. The building was L-shaped, so part of the dining room was not visible. He didn't see bearded Waterman, nor the blonde.

"There's a booth over there." Mary strode to the left.

"Partially hidden behind a wall and near the restrooms?"

"Might be kind of convenient," she said and rubbed her lower stomach. "I like the country atmosphere, the mismatched dishes under gingham cloths. The wooden chairs and fake daisies on the tables add ambience. I'm sure the food is so good, you won't notice the bathrooms."

She was hungry, so he'd ignore the fact the seating wasn't a prime spot for dining or for viewing the entrance.

"All right. Lead the way."

Her cute derriere wiggling, she forged a path to the booth. She slid onto the seat facing the restroom, which placed him toward the entrance and exit. Instead of scooting to the middle of the soft red bench, he stayed near the edge, keeping a partial view of the door in sight. No doubt the blonde would be coming into the restaurant, and he'd be ready when she arrived.

Mary had settled on the low dipping seat, straightened her blouse, and focused on the faded yellow rose-embossed wallpaper. He loved her. Regardless of what her intent had been on the cruise ship, he'd forgive her, and hopefully after the threat to her life had been resolved, they could build a relationship together. A family.

"Hello." The server's lacy name badge indicated she was Ida. She held a black round tray in her hand. She slid two glasses of water onto the table without spilling a drop and placed a basket of yeast biscuits dead center. The fresh, delicious aroma made all his qualms about the restroom disappear. However, not having a good visual on the front entrance bothered him. He'd encourage Mary to shove the food down, and they'd be out the door within minutes.

"Here are a couple of menus. Today's specials are beef brisket, fresh salmon, or if you're inclined, waffles with authentic maple syrup. What would you like to drink?" Two bread plates clicked as they connected with the crystal. Ida switched the tray to rest under her arm.

"Glass of milk." Mary shrugged out of her coat. Regardless of his sweatshirt underneath, he planned to leave his jacket on for a little longer. His blood was southern thin.

"Coffee for me." John glanced into Ida's sparkling blue eyes. A slight grin indicated she saw something. Was his love for Mary so obvious even a server, a stranger, read his emotions? He had to get off field duty. Some of his skills sucked.

"I'll give you two a few minutes to decide." Ida's voice softened, from business let's-get-this-done to sweet and motherly.

Mary tore into a biscuit and dropped the two halves on the plate. She smeared butter on top. "She's nice."

"Yes." He couldn't get the words to exit his mouth. No number of interrogations or lessons in public speaking would help him during this intimate conversation.

The bread dripped butter as she squeezed it between her lips. Eyes closed, she moaned, a soft, sexy sound. She hadn't opened her eyelids as she delicately chewed. John could almost hear whimpers coming from down deep in her throat. Finished crunching, she licked her lips. His cock pressed against the cotton of his Dockers, and he knew if she repeated the action, with a louder groan, he'd explode right there in the tiny booth.

"This is good, you should try one." She took a sip of her water.

He met her gaze.

"Oh." She coughed into her napkin. "John, I've something--"

"Have you decided?" Ida held a steaming carafe and a coffee cup in one hand and a glass of milk in the other. She placed the tumbler in front of Mary and poured the coffee. John briefly glanced at her, the main door, and then at Mary.

"Maybe I should come back in a few minutes?"

"Yes, thank you, Ida," he replied, shifted the coffee to the right, and folded his hands on the dark green checkered cloth.

Having finished the biscuit half, Mary took a drink of the milk and wiped her mouth with the soft paper. She played with the toggle on her purse.

A server refreshed the coffee for the people in the next booth.

Was Mary ready to announce the undisclosed? A secret he was afraid he already knew. "You were saying?"

He added a smile, a reassuring grin to let her know whatever the announcement, she was safe with him.

* * * *

Mary cleared her throat. The time was right to tell him the truth. She'd unconsciously tricked him, and now he was going to be a father. *Just say it.* Let the conception announcement become the bandage, and with one swift zip, the fear of pain, of the unknown, would be over. But what if he thought she'd used him to get with child? She hadn't, maybe in her subconscious, but not outright. Conrad frightening her in the hallway had scared her into thinking she'd never be able to act on the donor list. At dinner she'd drunk wine, which sealed her acceptance that conception was a thing of the past.

John, unlike any other man she'd ever been attracted to, didn't meet her dating criteria. He had dark hair, brown eyes and golden skin. His high intellect and determination scared her. She closed her eyes. Their children would be undeniably beautiful!

He waited, not saying anything, not distracted by the pungent coffee filtering into the air between them. His penetrating stare made her throat shut.

She gasped for breath, dreading the outcome. "Did I tell you my mother, Laurie, was a member of a circus act before she met my father?"

He shook his head and a glint of amusement rippled across his eyes. "No."

"She was a knife thrower, with The Cutting Edge, and exceedingly good." She swallowed. "Family business. I still have some distant cousins tossing the blade. My mother always claimed that she scared the sperm out of my father, which was the reason she couldn't have another child." Mary winked. "They argued a lot. The older they got and the longer they were together, the friendly disagreements became more frequent."

"You were an only child because of procreation problems?" Apparently unable to resist the scent of the coffee, he wove a finger through the loop on the mug and took a sip.

"Yes. Last year I discovered I had reproduction issues." She licked her lips. "I was under fertility management when my boyfriend robbed the bank."

John let go of the cup. The jerky movement spilled coffee on the table. "Sorry. Clumsy."

He quickly cleaned the hot liquid, using a napkin. "So your visit today was because you found out you're pregnant."

Her heart beat faster than the drip coffee maker a few feet away. The gallon of water she'd drunk so she could pee in a cup at the doctor's office suddenly pressed against her bladder. Crap, her show and tell wasn't going well. He probably thought she got pregnant by her loser ex. "Yes, I'm four weeks pregnant."

His fists tightened on the napkin. "The bartender?"

Abort. Abort conversation right now. "Why would you say such a thing?"

For the first time since she'd known John Kajiyama, his face flushed red, and his eyes narrowed to slits. "Because of the sperm donor list. I wasn't a candidate."

Her worst fears were spread out on the table. "Excuse me. I need to use the facilities."

"Mary," he said, a beseeching quality to his tone.

She bent and picked up her fallen coat, stuffing it on the seat. With shaking hands, she tossed the shoulder strap of her purse over her arm and hurried to the women's restroom.

Chapter 23

John hit the table with his fist. Ceramic dishes rattled and his spoon clinked as it smashed against the wooden floorboards. He held onto the cup. Uncomfortable with the couple staring at him from the next booth, he bent to pick up the fallen silverware. A flash of red appeared in the corner of his vision, an older woman with bright white-blond hair.

He came upright in time to see the women's restroom door close. Damn. A quick glance around the restaurant didn't prove someone had left a black coat on a chair. He ran to the entrance, stepped out. The navy van was parked near the street. The vehicles were covered with snow. Damn, what kind of protector was he?

Pivoting, he returned inside. Ida held the tray under her arm and chatted with a couple of bearded men at a table. "Ida, did you see a woman, blond hair, black overcoat and red dress?

"Yep, her and your wife just walked out the side door." Ida pointed her bright crimson fingernail toward the restrooms.

"Fuck! Ida, call the police. Kidnapping." His heart hurt and his breathing had stopped, so he prayed he could run. His legs carried him forward. He whipped his Glock from the hard leather of his shoulder holster and threw open the creaky wood door leading outside.

Mary struggled with the woman. She dug her fingers into the attacker's coat and repeatedly kicked her heel against the kidnapper's shin.

John ran forward. "Let go of her."

The woman let go of Mary's arm and twisted, so only her side was visible.

"Mary, run!" John's shooting average was decent, not sharpshooter perfect. Regardless, he'd take the kidnapper down. But the woman still held Mary. Their frosty breaths clouded the air. The click of his safety being disengaged vibrated off the metal of the cars.

"John!" Mary screamed. She hadn't moved.

"Go."

"She can't, there's a .38 pointed directly in line with her stomach. Our little jewel thief moves one inch, and *bang*." The aggressor made a slicing motion in the air. Her voice was deep, and an Adam's apple moved as she spoke. Without a wig and breasts, the attacker would match Waterman's mug shot.

"Where's the diamonds, bitch?" Waterman asked.

"I'll take you to them, just don't hurt me." Mary met John's gaze, then nodded toward the ground.

"We'll work out a deal, Waterman, if you let her go." John centered on the kidnapper's shoulder, holding steady.

Mary jerked, glanced at John, and then fell backward. Supported by a fender, she didn't hit the ground.

Waterman bent. John let off a shot and hit the cross-dresser exactly where he'd aimed. Waterman dropped the gun and screamed like a banshee. Arms outstretched, he scuttled toward his vehicle.

Heart racing, John rushed forward.

A knife sliced through the air, sticking into Waterman's forearm like a hunk of meat being cleaved.

Mary's hand dropped, and then she fell to the snow-blanketed pavement.

* * * *

John flipped on the desk lamp in an attempt to fight off the gloom of darkness. Late afternoon, the day before Thanksgiving, the Atlantic Coast Investigation Florida offices were vacant. The other agents and staff had left early to travel, or welcome loved ones into their homes.

Loved ones! The regular beat of his heart suddenly stopped as if a mini-death had occurred. Mary was the one he loved. Upon release from the emergency room, she'd insisted on returning to Bushard's guest house.

The next day John had escorted her to South Carolina. No soft endearments were spoken. After her collapse he was afraid of her fragility, so he didn't bring up the subject of the baby or, regrettably, his love for her. She'd slept on the plane and her grandfather had met her at the airport. Her sad eyes had held a glint of hope. They had to talk.

Two days had passed before John crashed on his sofa in Fort Myers, and slept for a solid sixteen hours. He'd dreamed of her. Not of her being attacked by the two men, or in a hospital room, but of her walking into his apartment. She'd greet him with a kiss and say she'd missed him and they'd snuggle like lovers.

He had been a fool to imagine such a romantic scenario. She'd misled him about the diamonds and used him to obtain what her heart desired. The ER doctor had warned her to rest. Was she taking care of their baby?

John shook his moroseness aside, left the cold empty office, and drove to his equally barren home. For the tenth time, he reviewed the cruise ship's security footage, watching for her reaction to each public encounter, paying particular attention to when they were together. Her eyes expressed her thoughts, in contradiction to her body language.

She fell into his cabin and into his arms. At the time, he couldn't get past her floral scented soft skin and perfect perky nipples. Today he looked beyond the obvious, noted her surprise and exhaustion. She'd hit the cruise ship running and hadn't stopped her trot until a few days ago.

Relieved of any responsibility for the theft, she'd been released. He'd see her again at the trials, but currently she was worry free. Her grandfather had been cordial. He'd given her a hug, but he seemed cold and distant. John considered calling, but why hadn't she contacted him? Since his outburst at the restaurant in Cage, Vermont, they'd exchanged a few simple words and no promises of tomorrow. Where was she now? In her home in Keefe, with her friends surrounding her?

John rewound the tape to the night he'd kissed Debbie on the cruise, a mean, vindictive attempt to get Mary's attention. Mary had casually unlocked her cabin door, but her green eyes had shot bolts of fire. He chuckled. If only he'd noticed her jealousy at the time. The trip would have played out differently, because they would have spent the entire night in bed, and she wouldn't have been accosted by Conrad.

Conrad Peabody. John dug out a cruise tape labeled *Hallway, Lower level, Portside* and quickly found the footage of Mary running. The attacker kept hidden in the shadows, but a glint of silver flashed across the screen. He'd sectioned a full face view and matched the dimensions to the mug shot and robbery profiles. If he'd had more time, he could have built trust with Mary. She would have told him about Peabody and the hallway assault. He could have taken Conrad out before she'd been cut.

John rolled his chair an inch to the right and swirled the mouse, advancing to the video clip of the day the hit went down. Although Mary fluttered her hands in apparent joy of having a trip into Kingston, her eyes held sadness. Had she wanted to leave him? Was he pipe dreaming her desire because he wanted her to love him? To stay with him?

He left the freeze frame of her eyes on the screen.

What was she doing now? Would she talk to him? A few punches with his index finger to the phone pad, and Mary's voice rang through the line. "Leave a message after the tone."

He found Phoenix's contact information in his database, picked up his cell, and dialed her home phone number.

* * * *

Mary stared at her pay-as-you-go cellphone, wishing it would ring. She snipped a piece of silver wire with her cutters. A little hard, as the short end pinged against the metal bookcase beside her. *Forget him. Focus on the medium flow point.* She was in Devon's son's workroom and didn't want to damage anything. The room's style--cold contemporary metals and sharp lines--wasn't her taste, but was the perfect set up for her temporary jewelry design station. She applied the flux, because she didn't want ugly oxides to form when she heated the angel wings.

Holiday Buckness by J Crew jingled from her phone. She pressed the speaker. "Hi, Phoenix. Are you on the road?"

"Yes. Another hour and I'll be there. Are you okay?"

"Yeppers. Just making angels." Forcing joy into her voice, she twisted a bit of wire into a wing shape. She inhaled the fresh woodsy scents. She and Devon had decorated the room with Christmas cheer the night before.

"Your voice doesn't match your words. I could kill Kajiyama. What was he thinking, questioning your morals? You don't sleep around." The angry tone in Phoenix's voice made Mary smile.

"But that was the reason I went on the cruise ship, was it not?" Mary picked up the webbed wire mesh and carefully soldered the ends to the wing. She didn't need pins for this portion of the structure, due to its simple free form. "Phoenix, he really doesn't know me, and he figured out the donor list. I can understand how he could jump to that conclusion."

The pain from those few words was as sharp as insect pins inserted into her heart. John wouldn't have believed the child was his, because he didn't trust her. It was probably for the best that she hadn't talked to him since the announcement of her condition.

"Are you kidding me? The bastard had researched you, prepared to... damn. I need to call you back. There's a bus in front of me with rowdy teens hanging from the window. For heaven's sake, it's snowing." Phoenix clicked off, ending the call.

After pressing *End* on her cell, Mary lifted her wrist and wiped her eyes. Despite telling herself to be strong and not to let John's attitude bother her, tears trailed down her cheeks and her heart hurt.

"Baby, I'm sorry, but it'll just be you and me," she said, massaging the slight mound of her stomach. Focus. Time passed quickly as she worked. She dipped the wing in the pickling solution, and sniffed. The pungent aroma of the non-toxic cleaner rose into the air. Mary wound the tweezers between her fingers as the metal heated in the deep glass tray.

"Don't you usually work with music on?" Devon asked from behind her.

She dragged her sleeve across her eyes as she turned to face him. "You betcha. Turn on the MP3 player for me. Something happy and fast. The docking station and those Belkin speakers are of the highest quality. I'm glad your kid has all the latest and greatest."

He snorted.

Leona Lewis's deep, throaty voice rang through the room, singing about heartbreak. Fantastic! Just what she needed, a frickin' bleeding heart song.

"Why don't you get some rest?" Devon took in her face and body, then narrowed his gaze on her eyes.

They must look like crap, all red and swollen from the weep fest. She couldn't lift her hand to wipe away the misery, because that would confirm his obvious suspicions.

"Do you cry in relief the case has been resolved and you can return to the ordinary treadmill of work, or because of him?" Devon didn't sneer as Phoenix would have, although his perfect lips formed into a frown.

She'd avoid the truth, and ignore Leona's heartbreak. "I've decided to stay. Get a little house and continue to work for Frank at the Garden Center." A gentle shove, and the second stool went toward Devon.

He took the seat. "I'd love that. And the community will too. What about your friends in South Carolina?"

"Ah, I can tell Phoenix has been sharing tales." Mary affixed the wing to the body of the angel and prepared the second one.

A short chuckle erupted from his chest. "Only the good ones. I'm hoping you'll give me the never-tell-anyone stories."

"We've a tight bond, my sisters-in-life and I. I tell no secrets."

"That's obvious by your avoidance of my question." He touched her arm, his fingers warm. She shut off the torch and laid it on the tabletop. "I've done work for many a DC bureaucrat. Give me the word, and I'll make a ruckus."

She bent her head as her heart ramped into hyper drive. He was so thoughtful and considerate. They had bonded so quickly, more than likely because his wife was killed by a robber and Mary's life had been severely affected by a jewel thief.

Devon lifted her chin. "Mary?"

She could barely see through the tears covering her eyes. "Why couldn't we have fallen in love?"

"You take the prize." With his index finger, he moved over her scar. "Jackknife did a good job on the stitches."

Mary teasingly shoved his hand away and turned back to her makeshift workbench. Leona had ended her song and Mary felt as if she were the one who should seal the cut. Her stomach flipped. Before she finished the angel, she needed to get a drink of milk to settle the acid. Deception and heartache were never easy to accept.

She lifted the wing and held it to the wire body. "How did Dr. Secreast get the nickname Jackknife?"

"Jackknife will wait. You are not avoiding me any longer. Do I make the call, or do you truly love John Kajiyama?"

Her throat closed, and her heartbeat pulsed heavily in her throat. Could she say the words aloud? By announcing her adoration, would the emotion be validated, and she'd add another charm to her wrong-choice boyfriend bracelet?

Mary dropped the angel in the solution and swiveled on the chair. Devon's dreamy blue eyes pierced her already pain-filled core. "Would it make a difference in my future if I had fallen in love with him?"

Devon drew her close. "Yes, honey, it does make a difference. The poor man's in love with you too. He's blinded by the whole stupid list you and your friends devised."

He released her head, smoothed her hair, and rested his slender surgically-divine fingers on her shoulder. "I'm sure the poor sap is looking for you as we speak and none of your loyal friends will tell the guy where to find you."

A song about broken glass ripped through the room. Leona was right; it was difficult to walk on broken glass. A tear fell off her cheek, and he caught the crystal drop with precision.

"He'll never look for you at my house, so what do we do?" Devon asked.

The doorbell chimed, relieving her of the need to answer. "Phoenix has arrived. Turn the music up before you and my best friend get it on. I don't want my baby to have any knowledge of sexual moans and groans before she's twenty-one."

Chuckling, he increased the volume and fled as if he were a teen instead of a man in his mature years.

"Will I ever have a man jump for joy at seeing me?" Mary asked, without expecting an answer. She put her supplies away, checked to make sure all the appliances were turned off and headed to the guest wing of the house.

Chapter 24

John stood near the front entrance and peered through the windows, not as a voyeur, but intending to see if Mary was inside. A couple danced in the dimly lit room. The outline of a woman, larger breasts, a waist so tiny a man's hands could span it and a decent bootie. Her red dress billowed out, the same dress she'd worn on the cruise ship. Devon lowered his head to the side of her neck. A tinkling laugh flowed through the window. Rage like John had never experienced before slashed through him, burning a path into his throat. His eyes watered from the pain.

Unwilling to window-peep and envy the man holding the woman of his dreams, John pivoted and headed down the sidewalk to his car. He clasped the lever, pulled, and then glanced at the white contemporary house with perfectly shaped evergreen shrubs lining the perimeter. Impossible. She wouldn't make love with him and days later dance hip to hip with Devon Buckley.

John slammed the door, hard enough to rock the Beemer, then rushed along the concrete sidewalk before he could change his mind. The loud *ding dong* vibrated beneath his fingertip as he pressed the bell button. The woman from the window appeared, her hand remaining on the knob as if ready to slam the entrance shut at a moment's notice. His heart thwacked, fast and hard against his chest bone. Relief didn't make the pounding slow down.

"Who is it, honey?" Devon shouted from the background.

"The bastard who broke Mary's heart," Phoenix said, with enough anger in her voice to make any sane man quake.

"Good evening, Phoenix. I need to see her, talk with her." To keep from throwing the door open and looking for Mary himself, John shoved his hands into his pockets.

"I can't believe I told her to open her heart and let you in. What was I thinking?" Phoenix slammed her hand against the frame. "I should have gone with the bartender. He wouldn't have left her cold."

"Could I talk to her, please?" John would not give up.

Phoenix inched the door closed, attempting to shut him out. "She's not here, and I'm not going to tell her you're looking--"

"Jennifer told me she was here," John insisted.

Devon appeared behind Phoenix and rested a hand on her shoulder. "She'll be at Landware's dinner party tomorrow. It takes place at one."

"Thanks, Devon."

* * * *

Real estate in upper Vermont was the topic of discussion between Mrs. Landware and her cousin's youngest son, Drew. Nauseous and bored, Mary glanced around the foyer. New up-lights strategically placed around the Christmas tree illuminated the handcrafted ornaments. The beige marble floor gleamed under a two tiered chandelier. Christmas music piped through surround sound. Currently, *Silent Night* titillated her ear drums. It was all too much. She wanted to leave.

Mrs. Landware, Drew and two of her other relatives stood in the waiting area. A late lunch would be served in half an hour. Sadness weighted her. She couldn't wait for the day to end, and more importantly for her heartache to ease. But that would take time, if it ever happened. The scent of cinnamon, cloves and fresh baked bread made her stomach growl. She flattened her hands below her waist, feeling the slight baby-bump. A rush of joy that her child had finally made an outward appearance, in mound form, made her lips curve upward.

"Yes, I'd smile too, Mary. You did a fantastic job. Don't you agree, Drew?" Mrs. Landware held onto her cousin's arm as if she needed a crutch.

Drew's round face flushed red. He straightened his elf-embossed green vest, and then the tie boasting large red cherries topping off the colorful arrangement. He kept sliding his fingers along his heavy thighs, as if out of habit. Soon he found a place to rest his hands inside his trouser pockets. "Yes, she is beautiful. I mean, yes, the decorations are beautiful."

Mary felt a wave of sympathy for his nervousness The ring-a-ling of the doorbell gave her brief relief from the uncomfortable silence.

Without losing the rhythm of her conversation, one of the cousins opened the door.

John entered, wearing a frown and a three-piece dark suit. Immediately Mary met his gaze. She wanted to turn away, but couldn't. Her womb clutched in joy. Despite her disappointment, she loved John Kajiyama, the forever kind of love she'd always been searching for but had never found. Until now.

"John, welcome, come join us," Mrs. Landware said, her voice lifting to the top of the twelve-foot ceiling and across the foyer. Her bejeweled fingers flagged him.

Jaw unclenched, he strode toward the threesome, keeping his gaze on Mary. Her breath stopped and tears threatened to spill. Fortunately, he shifted his glance to their host and handed her a bunch of hot house flowers.

"Thank you for the invitation, Dorothy." John's deep voice sent quivers through Mary's body from the tips of her fingers to the ends of her toes.

"Thanksgiving wouldn't be a day of celebration if I didn't have my two favorite decorators here," Dorothy said, and carried the bouquet to her nose.

"You're a decorator?" Drew asked. A ridiculing glimmer appeared in his eyes.

"John, this is my cousin, Drew Oran. Drew, meet John Kajiyama, Mary's partner." Mrs. Landware's eyes glittered with mischief.

"I'd thought she was to be my date?" Drew stage whispered.

"Come along Drew, and I'll show you how to arrange blooms in a vase." Mrs. Landware pressed his arm, then turned around and glanced upward. "There is mistletoe. According to Norse legend, the mistletoe is a symbol for love and a kiss seals the magic."

A sly wink, and she moved Drew and the other two people along.

"Hi!" John took Mary's hand.

"What are you doing here?" Her voice came out soft and weepy, so she added a hard edge on the last word.

"I reviewed the tapes from the ship--"

She jerked her hand away. "Spying on me every minute wasn't enough?"

His fingers grasped her arms. "Wait, I'm going about this all wrong. I love you."

Mary took a step back, increasing the space between them.

"Please, let me explain." John closed the distance, encircled her waist and took a deep breath. "Shouldn't we honor the mistletoe?" he whispered, and glanced upward. She'd stepped directly beneath it.

Love. John had said he loved her. Her heart plunged upward and outward, beating against her breast. She couldn't seem to draw breath and wanted so badly to move away, but his kisses were tiny drops of heaven.

He loved her. Her shoulders relaxed, and she nodded. "It might be wrong to break with tradition."

With shaking hands, she rested her wrists on his shoulders and allowed her belly to expand. He must have noticed, as his grip on her back relaxed and he commenced rubbing soothing circles. "Magic should continue."

According to Mrs. Landware, the mistletoe was recognized for creating a spell of enchantment, and when John kissed her, sparks of magic did surround them. The love she felt for him rose from the bottom of her toes straight into her throat, making it difficult to breathe.

"John."

"Yes, love." His hips touched hers, and they danced, moving in time to *Edelweiss*, now filling the foyer.

"You weren't on my donor list because you weren't a by-your-leave, sex only encounter. I had fallen in love with you."

He drew a sharp breath. "Had?"

"Do. I do love you."

"Magical mistletoe." Crystal sparkled and the tiny pointed edges of the leafy greens hung over their heads. The song ended and John stopped. Waiting for the kiss, she wet her lips.

"Please be my wife, Mary Keefe. Let's start a life together, raise a family and decorate trees with our own special memories."

"Yes, I'll marry you," she said, and kissed him.

Meet the Author

Deeply moved by a niece's heartbreaking story of her inability to conceive a child and other stories of couples who experienced difficulty getting pregnant, I wrote *Jewel Heist*.

Conception problems can be distressing, not to mention destructive to a marriage and a woman's self-esteem. Sometimes the condition has a simple solution, while some require medical hi-tech involvement.

As I listened to my family members discuss the process and their success and failure rates, I became more intrigued.

The story began to form as I worked with glass and jewels to create works of art, or "crafts" as my husband would claim. For the heroine I used my background knowledge about jewelry design.

Mary's plight is heart wrenching, and John's desire to do what is right as he falls in love--sympathetic.

jj's Website:
http://twitter.com/jjKellerauthor
https://www.facebook.com/jj.keller.58
http://romancewithjjkeller.wordpress.com

Reader eMail:
justjkeller@yahoo.com